He gave her a look that said she was pushing her luck.

Raine heard him swear under his breath as he walked away. She watched him, trying to gauge what kind of man he really was. One thing was for sure, he had no idea who the woman he'd just taken captive really was.

As she watched him, for the first time, she took a good look at Cordell Winchester. She was suddenly aware of the man on some primitive level. He looked like an ad for Montana, a cowboy who was just as comfortable in the wild outdoors as in a large city or a boardroom. She must have been blind not to have noticed before this how his jeans hugged his tight behind, the legs long, the hips slim.

Raine felt desire warm her blood. It had been a long time since she'd been even remotely aware of a man. She'd been too busy with her career. She'd apparently forgotten what it felt like to want a man so much it made her ache. Or maybe she'd just never known a man like Cordell, a man who could unleash that kind of primal need even when she couldn't stand the sight of him.

This was a man who had to be used to getting what he wanted from women. She was glad she wasn't that type of woman. But the thought also came with a little regret that she wouldn't be finding out if Cordell Winchester was as sexy as he looked.

B.J. DANIELS

TWELVE-GAUGE GUARDIAN

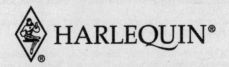

HARLEQUIN®

TORONTO • NEW YORK • LONDON
AMSTERDAM • PARIS • SYDNEY • HAMBURG
STOCKHOLM • ATHENS • TOKYO • MILAN • MADRID
PRAGUE • WARSAW • BUDAPEST • AUCKLAND

This book is dedicated to mothers.
Please warn your children not only about strangers but what to do if they are approached by them. We need to keep our little ones safe.

Recycling programs
for this product may
not exist in your area.

ISBN-13: 978-0-373-69477-8

TWELVE-GAUGE GUARDIAN

www.eHarlequin.com

Printed in U.S.A.

ABOUT THE AUTHOR

B.J. Daniels wrote her first book after a career as an award-winning newspaper journalist and author of thirty-seven published short stories. That first book, *Odd Man Out,* received a four-and-a-half-star review from *RT Book Reviews* and went on to be nominated for Best Intrigue for that year. Since then she has won numerous awards, including a career achievement award for romantic suspense and many nominations and awards for best book.

Daniels lives in Montana with her husband, Parker, and two springer spaniels, Spot and Jem. When she isn't writing, she snowboards, camps, boats and plays tennis. Daniels is a member of Mystery Writers of America, Sisters in Crime, International Thriller Writers, Kiss of Death and Romance Writers of America.

To contact her, write to B.J. Daniels, P.O. Box 1173, Malta, MT 59538 or e-mail her at bjdaniels@mtintouch.net. Check out her Web site at www.bjdaniels.com.

Books by B.J. Daniels

CAST OF CHARACTERS

Cordell Winchester—The private investigator thought he could never trust again until he tangled with the right woman.

Raine Chandler—She'd come to Whitehorse looking for answers never expecting to meet the man of her dreams.

Cyrus Winchester—He would never hesitate to help a woman in distress…even if it cost him his life.

Pepper Winchester—She had her reasons for inviting her family back to the ranch, none of them included her dying.

Virginia Winchester—The first one to return to the ranch, she'd believed her mother was dying and didn't want to be left out of the Winchester fortune.

Brand Winchester—He'd only come back to Whitehorse because he'd heard that one of his twin sons was in trouble.

Worth Winchester—What choice did he have but to come back to the ranch if his other siblings were there?

Emily Frank—She was ten the day she was snatched off the road on her way home from school in Whitehorse.

Orville Cline—The convicted child abductor confessed to killing Emily Frank, so why would anyone think he'd lied?

Grace and Abel Amberson—The couple felt called to be foster parents and still grieved over the one child they felt they'd failed.

Adele and Bill Beaumont—They'd always wanted children of their own, but after thirty-six years of marriage had accepted they would never be parents.

McCall Winchester—The acting sheriff found herself a little too busy to be planning her Christmas wedding at Winchester Ranch.

Chapter One

Cordell Winchester almost missed the Whitehorse Hotel. The old four-story brick building sat in a grove of cottonwoods on the far edge of town, the morning sun glinting off the worn structure.

More than a hundred years old, the place looked deserted. He took note of the vacant surroundings as he parked and went inside. The first thing that struck him was the aging smell, reminding him unpleasantly of his grandmother's lodge. It wasn't a reminder he needed this morning.

He'd been seven the last time he'd seen the Winchester Ranch—twenty-seven years ago—but he recalled the rambling old place only too well. He had always thought nothing could get him back to Whitehorse—let alone to the ranch.

The hotel lobby was done in overstuffed couches and chairs, the upholstery fabrics as dated as the furniture. At the unoccupied registration desk, he rang the bell, then turned to look toward the small parking area outside. No sign of his brother's black pickup.

Where was Cyrus? Not at Winchester Ranch. Cordell

had called out there and their grandmother hadn't seen or heard from him. So where the hell was he?

Cordell took off his Stetson and raked a hand through his thick dark hair as he studied the small Western town in the distance. At a sound, he spun around to find an ancient man had appeared behind the counter as if out of nowhere.

"May I help you?" asked the stooped, gray-headed old man.

"My brother Cyrus Winchester is staying with you," he said, settling the Stetson back on his head.

The man nodded, showing no sign of surprise at seeing Cyrus's identical twin. Clearly this man hadn't checked in his brother last night. The clerk thumbed through a file with gnarled fingers. "412. Shall I ring him for you?" He'd already picked up the phone and dialed the room.

Just as Cordell had expected, Cyrus didn't answer. He'd been trying his brother's cell since late last night and gotten no answer and Cyrus's truck was missing. A sure sign Cyrus wasn't here.

Cordell wished now that he'd insisted his brother wait and they ride together, but Cyrus wanted to leave a few days earlier and stop to see friends in Wyoming. Cordell had been tied up with a case and couldn't leave until yesterday. He'd flown into Billings, spent the night and had driven the rest of the way this morning.

He and Cyrus had planned to go out for breakfast when he arrived, where Cordell had planned to make one last attempt to try to talk his brother out of this visit to their grandmother.

"I'm afraid there is no answer in his room."

"Did you happen to see him leave?" Cordell asked even though he figured that was doubtful. The parking area, he'd noticed when he'd driven in, was at the back of the hotel. The clerk couldn't see it from the front desk.

The old man's head wobbled back and forth. "I just came on duty."

"I'm worried about him." He couldn't put his finger on what had him so worried, but it was more than just being unable to reach his brother by phone since yesterday afternoon. "I'd like to check his room."

The elderly clerk hesitated.

Cordell took out his wallet, flashed his driver's license ID and Colorado private investigator license, explaining he was Cyrus's twin brother. He also laid a twenty on the counter. "I wouldn't ask except my brother hasn't been himself lately." Unfortunately true. Cyrus had been acting strangely since getting the letter from their grandmother's attorney inviting them back to the ranch.

The letter implied that their grandmother, Pepper Winchester, who'd spent the past twenty-seven years as a recluse, was dying and anyone who didn't come to the ranch would be exempt from a share of the legendary Winchester fortune.

Neither of them believed the fortune existed. And if it did, they weren't about to let their grandmother manipulate them with it. They'd seen the way their grandmother had used it to control their father and his brothers and sister.

But Cyrus had been insistent about wanting to go back to the ranch one last time. "Remember Enid and Alfred? I wonder if they're still alive. Come on, Cordell, haven't you ever wanted to see the ranch again?"

"No."

"Maybe I just want to see if that rambling old lodge is as scary as I remember it or the ranch is as vast as I recall."

Cordell didn't get it and said as much.

"You just don't want to go because Grandmother liked me best," his twin joked, a joke because their grandmother hadn't given a damn about any of her grandchildren even before she'd holed up at the ranch.

"I suppose it would be all right if you had a look in his room," the hotel clerk said now as he pocketed the twenty. He reached behind him and removed a key attached to an orange piece of plastic with the number 412 engraved on it and laid the key on the counter.

Cordell noticed that the other key to 412 was missing.

Rather than take the antiquated elevator, he ran up the stairs. He'd never liked small spaces. They reminded him of a room on the ranch that had been used as punishment when his father was a boy. The room had given him the creeps.

Just the thought made his stomach knot. What the hell was he doing here? Whitehorse, Montana, was the last place on earth he wanted to be. He had no desire to see his grandmother. Nor did he have any desire to return to the ranch and dredge up even some of the happier memories because, in his mind, the ranch was—if not haunted—then definitely cursed.

From the get-go, Cordell had had a bad feeling. That was why he hadn't been about to let Cyrus go out there alone. Cyrus and trouble just seemed to find each other.

And that was what had Cordell worried now. He should have heard from his twin by now.

At room 412, he knocked lightly as he studied the worn carpet under his boots. A warm breeze blew in through a window at the end of the hallway near the old-fashioned metal fire escape exit. The place smelled of decay and cleaner. It was just like Cyrus to pick a hotel like this to stay in, what his brother would have called "authentic."

He knocked again, a little louder this time just in case his brother had hung one on last night at the four bars in town and walked the half mile back from town, leaving his pickup wherever it had been parked.

"Cyrus," he called as he used the key and opened the door.

"He's not in there," said a female voice from down the hall.

Cordell turned to see an older woman with a cleaning cart.

"From the looks of his room, he didn't sleep here last night," she said and pursed her lips scornfully.

Cordell didn't like the sound of that and felt his anxiety multiply. He'd always "felt" his identical twin, sensed him on some cell-deep level even when they were miles apart.

He couldn't feel his brother. It was as if Cyrus was… The thought that his twin might be dead sent a gut-wrenching terror through him.

Pushing open the door to the room, he saw Cyrus's bag next to the undisturbed bed. The housekeeper was right. It didn't appear Cyrus had spent any time in the room other than to drop off his bag.

Moving through the small hotel room, he saw that his brother hadn't even dirtied a glass or broken the paper band on the toilet seat and his fear intensified.

Cordell pulled out his cell, saw that he hadn't received any calls from his twin, and started to call the ranch again when he spied Cyrus's cell phone on the table by the window.

Cyrus didn't go anywhere without his cell phone.

Heart pounding, he walked over and started to pick it up when he saw his brother's room key lying on the floor next to the wall where it must have fallen. Next to it was a paper convenience-mart cup on its side on the carpet in the middle of a dark stain that looked like spilled coffee.

Cordell fought to remain calm as he surveyed the scene, noticing that the curtain was pulled back, the window opened a few inches as if his brother had heard something and looked out and seen…what?

The room was located at the back of the hotel. A strip

of pavement made up the parking area. Beyond it was a stand of huge old cottonwoods that grew along what could have once been a ditch or creek.

Past that were piles of old lumber and scrap iron, and in the distance, Cordell could make out a weathered old run-down farmhouse. Several old cars were up on blocks and the yard was littered with toys. A bunch of sorry-looking kids were outside. They seemed to be hunting for something. He heard them calling for someone.

A large woman stood on the front steps of the farm-house, her hands on her hefty hips. She appeared to be giving the children orders in a strident voice.

Cordell turned his attention back to the parking lot below the window. He could see the glitter of glass on the patched pavement under the only light post. When his brother had arrived last night, it would have already been dark—especially in the parking lot without a light.

What could he have seen?

There were two cars parked between the faded painted lines, an old brown sedan with local plates and a blue VW bug with California plates. The VW had a flat tire on the left rear.

He stared at the flat tire unable to shake the bad feeling that had settled over him. Cyrus must have seen something down there last night. Something that had made him drop everything and run down to help?

He picked up his brother's cell phone and checked

to see if he'd gotten any messages other than Cordell's this morning, then checked Cyrus's outgoing calls.

Fear settled like a boulder in his belly when he saw that the last number his twin had called was 911.

Chapter Two

As Cordell started to look for a phone book to call the sheriff's department, he saw his brother's pickup coming up the road. Relief flooded him and yet at the same time he wanted to throttle his twin for scaring him like this.

He watched the pickup come in from a back way and wondered why he couldn't feel that connection that had always been there between the two of them.

It unsettled him and made him more anxious as he glanced at his watch. Cyrus was more than three hours late. Not only that, he'd also apparently spent the night elsewhere. It wasn't like his brother to have met a woman and been tom-cattin' around all night.

Cordell couldn't throw off the feeling that something had happened.

As the pickup pulled into the back lot and parked, he watched anxiously, just needing to see that his brother was all right.

The door of the pickup opened and with a start Cordell watched as a woman wearing a baseball cap over her short bluntly cut black hair climbed out. She was dressed in jeans, a jean jacket over a T-shirt and sneakers. Not really Cyrus's type, he thought.

Then she did something that sent a jolt through him.

She glanced nervously around the parking lot before her gaze shot up to the window where he stood. Cordell stepped back at the same instant and watched from behind the edge of the curtain as she opened the VW, took out something and seemed to stuff it under her jacket before heading for the back door of the hotel.

He quickly pocketed his brother's cell phone and room key and stepped into the closet, leaving the door open just enough that he could see most of the room.

It wasn't long before he heard voices out in the hall-way, both female. He knew without hearing all the conversation that the young woman driving his brother's truck had conned the maid into opening Cyrus's room for her.

He heard the door open, then close and lock. For a moment, she stood perfectly still as if listening, as well. Then she quickly moved to Cyrus's overnight bag on the end of the bed.

Cordell had a good view of her backside from where he was hidden. The woman appeared to be five-six or seven, slim with an athletic build and enough curves to fill out her jeans nicely. Had this woman been in trouble, Cyrus would have jumped to her defense without a second thought.

She unzipped the bag and hurriedly rummaged through it. He wondered what she was looking for. She definitely hadn't come to get something for his brother. So what was she doing with his pickup?

That was when he got a glimpse of the pistol stuck into the back waistband of her jeans. It peeked out from the hem of her jean jacket as she bent over the bag. Was that what she'd gotten out of the car?

Cordell moved swiftly, knowing the minute she heard the closet door roll back, she'd reach for the weapon.

She was fast, faster than he'd anticipated. Just not as fast as he was. He came out of the closet, diving for her and the weapon. At the sound behind her, she spun around, her hand going for the gun and coming out with it in her left hand.

As she swung toward him, leading with the weapon, he grabbed her wrist, driving her back and onto the bed. He wrenched the gun from her hand, tossing it across the room. It skittered to a stop near the door.

The woman got in a kick that only missed his groin by a couple of inches. Her right hook, though, caught him squarely in the jaw, surprising him by the force of her punch, before he could grab both her wrists and pin them and her to the bed.

Her eyes widened in alarm. *"You?!"* she cried, looking at him as if she'd seen a ghost and confirming that she'd at least seen his twin before she took his pickup.

"Where is my brother?" he demanded, holding her down on the bed.

"Your *brother?*" She stared at him as if dumbfounded.

"You're driving his pickup. You're in his room going through this stuff. Where is my brother?"

"I thought you—"

"I asked you a question." He knew what she thought. Few people could tell him and Cyrus apart.

Cordell pulled her arms up over her head, secured both wrists with one hand and reached for his cell phone. "You want to tell me or the sheriff? Your choice."

"Could you get off me? I can't breathe."

He studied her face. She was pretty but she hid it well with too much eye makeup along with a small silver nose ring and dyed black hair cut in a sleek bob that made her pale porcelain skin even paler.

"Come on. You're hurting me. Let me up and I'll tell you everything."

"I don't think so," he said, seeing something in her blue eyes that warned him this woman couldn't be trusted. "Let me say this again. My brother, where is he?"

As he started to dial 911, she said, "The last time I saw him, he was being taken to the hospital."

"The *hospital?* What happened to him?"

"I'm not sure. I think he was struck by a vehicle in the parking lot last night," she said, motioning with the snap of her head toward the back of the hotel.

The open drapes, the spilled coffee, Cyrus's cell phone on the table and the 911 call to the sheriff's department. Cordell felt his heart drop. "Is he all right?"

"I don't know."

Cordell shook his head in confusion. "Why did he go

down there unless… You! You didn't just witness this. You were involved somehow. How else did you get his pickup?" He could only assume his brother had rushed downstairs to save her. But from what?

She seemed to relent. "I was crossing the parking lot. I stopped, surprised to see that I had a flat tire on my car. Just then I heard an engine rev and this van came roaring out of the darkness."

"My brother saved you." It was the only thing that made sense. Cyrus must have seen the van and realized it was waiting for her.

"He shoved me out of the way. I fell. When I came to, a man who looks a lot like you was lying nearby." Her gaze skidded away. "I heard sirens. I didn't know what had happened. I was afraid the van would come back. I saw your brother's keys lying next to him and took his pickup."

"The sirens—"

"It was an ambulance," she said.

"Did you happen to notice while you were taking his keys if he was still alive?" Cordell asked with sarcasm that she seemed to ignore.

"He was still breathing from what I could tell."

Cordell couldn't hide his relief. "Nice of you to stick around and make sure he was all right."

She glared at him. "I'd had a scare. I didn't know your brother from Adam. For all I knew he was with the guys in the van."

He studied her. This whole mess sounded just like Cyrus. Maybe he'd even seen the driver of the van flatten her tire. The moment the man went back to his van to wait for her to come out of the hotel, Cyrus would have started to call 911. How, though, had the man in the van known she would come back out again last night?

"You'd just returned to the hotel? Wasn't it late?" he asked her. She looked surprised he'd figured that out. "So why leave again so soon?"

"I came back to check out. I'd changed motels."

"Why?"

"Isn't it obvious? I didn't like the feel of this place, too far from town and it's old and crumby."

Maybe she was telling the truth, though he had his doubts. He was still shaken by the news that his brother had been taken to the hospital after possibly being hit by a van to save this ungrateful woman's neck.

Fortunately Cyrus was tough. He would be all right. He had to. And yet that foreboding feeling was still with Cordell.

"So my brother saves you, first you take off and just leave him lying there and then you come back here to go through his belongings?"

"I'm not a thief," she snapped, her blue eyes darkening.

"What's your name?"

Again her gaze shifted away. "Raine Chandler."

"I'd like to see some identification."

She shot him a disbelieving look that said she'd couldn't show him anything with him on top of her.

He eased off and she reached as if to get something out of her hip pocket. The blow took him completely by surprise, knocking him back. As her fist connected with his nose, the pain radiating up through his skull, she wriggled out from under him. His vision blurred as his eyes filled. Blood poured from his nose as he reached for her.

But she was too fast. Through the film of tears, he saw her vault over the bed to the spot where he'd tossed her pistol by the door. She came up with the gun.

For a split second he thought she'd turn it on him. But then she was out the door.

He didn't try to stop her. A few moments later he heard her rev his brother's pickup engine and tear off, tires spitting gravel. No reason to give her chase. He was more concerned right now with getting to the hospital and seeing his brother.

Cyrus could deal with retrieving his pickup, Cordell thought as he went into the bathroom to clean himself up. He couldn't wait to hear his brother's side of the story. Downstairs, the hotel clerk gave him directions to the hospital.

"They're in the process of moving from the old hospital to the new one," the clerk told him.

It wasn't hard to find since the entire town of Whitehorse was only about ten blocks square. The new hospital was on the far east side of town in the opposite direction from the hotel where Cyrus had gotten a room he hadn't used.

When Cordell walked into the small reception area, the nurse behind the desk looked at him as if she'd seen a ghost. He'd gotten used to being an identical twin and often forgot about the effect it had on other people. They always did a double take when he and Cyrus were together.

When they were younger they played tricks on their teachers and even their girlfriends. The tricks often backfired, landing them in hot water.

Now as private investigators in Denver, he and Cyrus used being identical to their benefit. It was almost as if they could be in two places at one time.

Their grandmother had never been able to tell them apart, he remembered, then chastised himself for letting her creep into her thoughts. He knew he was just trying not to worry about Cyrus.

"I'm Cyrus Winchester's brother. Twin brother," he said to the nurse now as if that wasn't obvious.

"Oh," she said, both hands going over her heart. "You did give me a start when I saw you standing there." She patted herself as if trying to still that heart. "I thought, 'It's a miracle.'"

His stomach dipped. "A miracle?"

She seemed to realize what she'd said. "I'm sorry. Hasn't anyone told you? Of course not. Until you walked in here we didn't know the patient's name so we haven't been able to notify his next of kin. Your brother is in a coma and has been since he was brought in last night."

SOMEONE HAD BEEN in her room.

Raine realized it the moment she opened the motel-room door and saw the tiny piece of cardboard from the coffee cup she'd stuck in the jamb lying on the floor.

She froze, her gaze taking in the cheap motel room. She'd put the Do Not Disturb sign on the door and it was clear that the maid hadn't been in.

The bed was rumpled from the few hours of sleep she'd managed to get the night before and her towels were on the bathroom floor where she'd dropped them after a quick shower this morning.

She glanced behind the door, then at the open closet. She didn't like surprises and almost laughed out loud at the thought as she stepped cautiously in, pulling the pistol and closing the door and locking it silently behind her.

The room was small. Lumpy double bed, bathroom, closet. Not a lot of places for a person to hide. She checked under the bed, in the closet and behind the bathtub shower curtain. Empty.

Tucking the pistol back into the waist of her jeans, she checked her overnight bag. Someone had gone through it. What had they been looking for? Evidence, she thought. Or identification? She'd left neither in the bag.

Walking over to the window, she saw how they'd gotten in. The latch was broken on the sill. She'd planned to go to another motel tonight anyway. The window looked out on the alley, a stand of trees and an old house that had once been painted white.

Raine felt her pulse thrum in her veins and her heart began to pound at the sight of the aging house. She could almost smell the rank mustiness. She hated old houses.

Closing the curtain on both the window and the past, she quickly packed up the few belongings that she hadn't put in storage when she'd left home, then placed a call to a local car repair shop and made arrangements to have her flat tire fixed and her car brought into town, saying she would pick it up later.

She knew it was just a matter of time before that cowboy came looking for her. She was still shaken by her run-in with him at the hotel. He'd looked so much like the man she'd seen lying in the parking lot last night that it had taken her completely off guard.

Glancing around the room, she made sure she hadn't left anything, then walked to the door with her overnight bag in hand. She opened it a crack to look out. The hallway was empty.

She pulled the gun from her waistband and, unzipping her overnight bag, laid it on top, making the weapon more accessible should she need it.

As she pushed open the outside door, she scanned the parking lot. The lot was empty except for the pickup she was driving and a large, luxury car with Texas plates parked at the opposite end.

Trying not to hurry, she walked to the pickup, tossed in her bag and climbed in after it. For a moment, with the doors locked and the gun handy, she just sat, not sure what to do next.

Run. Just drive in any direction and get the hell out of here. She could dump the pickup somewhere down the road. Early this morning, she'd dug in the pickup's glove box looking for information on the man who'd shoved her out of the way of the van last night and had pulled up short when she'd seen who the truck was registered to. Cyrus Winchester of Winchester Investigations of Denver, Colorado.

What were the chances that the man who'd come to her rescue just happened to be a private eye?

She started the pickup but still didn't hit the road. She was kidding herself if she thought she could leave. Even if she had her car and had left this pickup where Cyrus's twin brother could find it, she couldn't run. She'd hate herself the rest of her life if she didn't follow through with this. Wasn't it time she learned the truth—not to mention got the justice she deserved?

Last night the parking area behind the old hotel had been too dark to see the person driving the van. But Raine figured he had to be the same one who'd slashed her tire. He'd been waiting for her.

You were set up, girl.

It certainly looked that way. But why had someone gone to the trouble of luring her to Whitehorse? Surely not just to run her down in the hotel parking lot. They could have killed her in L.A. since at least one of them obviously knew where to find her—and where to send the messages that had gotten her here in the first place.

Why, after all these years, try to kill her? It made no sense. They had no reason to believe anyone was after them. But now the sheriff's department would be looking for the dark-colored van because the driver had put Cyrus Winchester in the hospital.

And his brother would be looking for Raine. Finding her in a town the size of Whitehorse would be child's play—for both the cowboy *and* the attempted killer.

Any woman in her right mind would hightail it out of town and not look back.

But Raine Chandler wasn't just any woman, she thought with a curse.

Chapter Three

Cyrus looked pale, his head bandaged and a series of tubes and cords running from his lifeless body.

Cordell took his brother's limp hand in both of his and sat down hard on the chair next to the hospital bed. No wonder he'd felt the connection broken between them.

"Cy, I'm here," he said, his voice breaking. "I'm going to find out who did this to you and take care of it. In the meantime..." He glanced away from his brother's face, trying to compose himself. He didn't want his brother to hear the fear in his voice. "I just want you to rest so you can wake up soon."

He heard the scuff of a shoe sole behind him and turned to see the doctor standing in the doorway. He squeezed his brother's hand and, reluctantly letting go, rose.

"Tell me about my brother's condition," he said, motioning for the doctor to come out into the hallway with him. He didn't want to talk about it in front of Cyrus. He'd heard that comatose patients could hear what was being said to them and around them, and from the doctor's grave expression the diagnosis wasn't good.

"I'm Dr. Hanson," the elderly man said, searching Cordell's face. "Identical twins. You certainly gave my nurse a start." He grew more sober. "As she told you, your brother is in a coma. He was already comatose when he was brought in so we were unable to get any information from him."

"What caused the coma?"

"Blunt force trauma to the back of his head. There was also some bruising around the hip and left leg as if he'd been struck."

"Like being struck by a vehicle?" Cordell asked. "Apparently he pushed a woman out of the way of a speeding van. She didn't see what happened to Cyrus, but found him lying on the pavement."

The doctor nodded. "That would be consistent with his injuries."

Cordell had thought he would get the whole story from his brother once he reached the hospital. Now he saw that if he wanted to know any more about the accident he'd have to ask the woman. But first he had to make sure Cyrus was going to be all right.

"What can we do for him?" he asked the doctor.

"There appears to be no bleeding or swelling of the brain that requires surgery, but we will continue to monitor your brother closely. Right now he is stable, his vital signs strong. A coma rarely lasts more than two to four weeks."

Others last for years, Cordell thought. "I know my

brother. He's a fighter. He'll come out of this." Soon, he prayed.

The doctor gave him a sympathetic smile. "We certainly hope so. Some patients recover full awareness. Others require some therapy." His look said some were never the same. "We won't know the full extent of your brother's injury until he regains consciousness."

If he ever does. Cordell kept hearing the words the doctor *didn't* say. He felt helpless. But there was one thing he could do while he waited for his twin to come back and that was to get the bastard who'd done this to him.

That meant finding Raine Chandler, and getting the truth out of her.

As RAINE DROVE THROUGH a residential neighborhood in Whitehorse, she pulled out her cell phone and hit a speed dial number, realizing she was calling in late.

"I was just about to call out the cavalry," Marias drawled.

"Sorry, I've been a little busy."

"Uh-huh." Her friend had been against her coming to Whitehorse from the get-go. "What happened?" Marias knew her too well.

"I ran into a little trouble last night, but I'm fine."

"They know you're there *already?*" Marias let out an unladylike oath. But then there was nothing ladylike about the biker-turned-cop-turned-P.I.

"Not a huge surprise under the circumstances. I'm not sure where I'm going to be staying so I might not be able to get Internet or cell phone coverage. Seriously," she said when Marias snorted in disbelief. "Whitehorse is in the middle of nowhere and once you get outside the city limits, all bets are off when it comes to high-tech devices."

"You're leaving?" Just like Marias to latch on to that.

"No, just maybe staying outside town if I can find a place." Up the block, Raine spotted a tan sedan like the one she'd seen behind the hotel this morning. The car was parked in front of the new hospital. Of course he would go see how his brother was doing and his brother would tell him everything.

He would find out she'd been telling the truth. She hoped that would be the last she'd see of the cowboy.

Unless, of course, he and his P.I. brother were somehow involved. What if the plan last night hadn't been to kill her but to save her? She would have been indebted to Cyrus Winchester. Maybe something had gone wrong and instead of saving her, he'd ended up in the hospital.

And now his identical twin was putting the strong arm on her.

A little paranoid, are you?

No, just covering all her bases, Raine thought. "I promise to try to stay in touch." She hung up before Marias could argue that this trip was nothing more than a suicide mission. If she only knew how complicated this had become.

Raine pulled over under a large tree next to a house

just down the block from the hospital. This might be the perfect opportunity to check out the car—and the man driving it.

She was about to get out of the pickup when she saw the twin come out and climb into the tan mid-size sedan. It had rental car written all over it. At least she'd been right about the car being the same one she'd seen parked behind the hotel this morning.

Sliding down in her seat, she peered through the steering wheel as he pulled out and headed toward downtown. Where was he going? She decided to follow at a safe distance and find out.

She was surprised though when the trail led to the sheriff's department. If last night's attack had been a ploy, then this cowboy wouldn't be going to the sheriff about it. He would want to keep all this as quiet as possible—and handle it himself.

She pulled over again and dialed information for Winchester Investigations in Denver, Colorado. The phone rang three times before a woman picked up and from the brisk way she answered, Raine guessed it was an answering service.

"I'm calling for Cyrus Winchester."

"I'm sorry, he's not available. Both Cyrus and Cordell Winchester are out of the office. If you'd like to leave a message—"

Raine hung up. *Both* Winchesters were private detectives? No way would a P.I. go to the cops unless he was on the up-and-up.

So what *were* they doing in Whitehorse?

THE WHITEHORSE COUNTY Sheriff's Department was located along the main drag in an old brick building. As Cordell climbed out of the rental car, he scanned the street.

In the diagonal parking spaces were a half-dozen trucks in front of the various businesses from a couple of bars and a café to a clothing store, beauty parlor, hardware and a knitting shop. None of the pickups were his brother's, though.

Inside the sheriff's department, Cordell spoke first to the dispatcher.

"I'll see if the sheriff is busy," she said.

He watched the street while he waited, feeling anxious. His fear was that the woman who'd called herself Raine Chandler would flee town. Her VW had California plates on it. What was she doing in Whitehorse? Apparently not just passing through. He'd had the good sense to take down the car's license plate, assuming it wasn't stolen. He wouldn't put anything past the woman given that she was toting a gun and clearly involved in something more than a near hit-and-run.

"Yes?"

He turned at the sound of a female voice to find an attractive dark-haired woman in a sheriff's uniform. Her head was cocked to one side as she perused him, her lips turning up into an amused smile.

"Which one are you?" she asked.

"I beg your pardon?"

"I'm sorry. I'm McCall Winchester, acting sheriff. I

recognized you from some photographs my grandmother showed me of you as a boy."

He caught her name and couldn't help frowning.

"Trace Winchester's daughter," she said.

He felt his eyes widen.

She let out a laugh. "Yes, I did turn out to be his daughter no matter what my grandmother said at the time. I'm the true black sheep of the family."

Cordell smiled at that. "It's a family of black sheep."

"Why don't we step back to my office?"

He followed her down the hallway, surprised that his cousin was the acting sheriff. She took a chair behind her desk and he settled into one of the others facing her. "My brother and I are up here because of our grandmother's letter."

McCall nodded. She didn't look happy about it.

"I'm guessing she isn't dying and wants something from us."

"That would be my guess," McCall agreed.

Cordell hadn't come here to talk about his grandmother and didn't give a damn what she was up to. He was too worried about Cyrus.

"Do you know about my brother's accident?" He saw that she didn't, probably because Cyrus hadn't had any identification on him. Which meant either the woman took Cyrus's wallet—or the van driver had stopped long enough to take it.

"Cyrus was attacked last night behind the Whitehorse Hotel. He's in a coma at the hospital."

"I'm so sorry. I'd heard a man had been injured and taken to the hospital but I had no idea it was your brother. The deputy on duty last night talked to the clerk who'd apparently called for an ambulance, but he said the only vehicle in the lot belonged to a woman."

Cordell nodded, thinking of the woman he'd tangled with earlier at the hotel. "The woman took my brother's pickup. She told me a crazy story about almost being run down by a person driving a dark-colored van. Her tire was flat on her VW, she said she was scared and saw Cyrus's keys on the ground and took off."

"So you talked to her?"

He looked away embarrassed that he'd let her go. "I was about to check her identification when she got away."

McCall raised an eyebrow at that. "I suppose that explains the blood on your shirt. It's yours?"

He looked down, not realizing some had dripped onto his sleeve. "She said her name was Raine Chandler, but I really doubt—"

"The VW bug with the flat behind the hotel is registered to a Raine Chandler of Los Angeles, California."

So she had been telling the truth—at least about that.

"Do you have some reason to doubt her story?" the sheriff asked.

Did he? Just a gut feeling that she was leaving out a whole lot of it. "I'm not sure. But with Cyrus in a coma, she is the only one who knows what really happened last night."

McCall frowned. "I heard that you and your brother are private investigators, but I hope you're not planning to take this matter into your own hands again. I'll put out an APB on her and your brother's pickup since she apparently didn't have permission to take his truck and she left the scene of an accident and possible crime last night."

"When you pick her up, I want to talk to her."

His cousin seemed to consider that. "I think we can work something out. I take it you haven't seen Grandmother yet."

"No."

"I'll let her bring you up to speed on everything that's been going on out there." His cousin shook her head as if whatever it was wasn't good.

Cordell rose from the chair, not bothering to tell her he had no intention of seeing Pepper Winchester. He had to find out who had injured his twin. He knew it was his way of dealing with Cyrus's coma. He told himself that by the time he found the bad guys and at least saw that they were behind bars, Cyrus would be all right again.

"It was nice meeting you." He reached into his wallet and took out his card. "My cell phone number is on there, but I'll check back with you."

RAINE CALLED MARIAS AGAIN. "I need your computer expertise. Can you check on a couple of private investigators out of Denver? The name is Winchester, Cordell and Cyrus Winchester of Winchester Investigations. See what you can find out."

"Anything special you're looking for?"

"Why they're in Whitehorse, Montana, would be helpful."

"I see. If you want to hang on… Do you happen to have a license plate number?" Marias asked.

"I can do better than that. I have Cyrus's pickup registration."

"I don't want to know, right?"

"Right." Raine reached over and opened the glove box. "Hold on, he's about to move again."

"He?"

"Cordell Winchester." From down the street, he had just come out of the sheriff's department. Raine leaned over out of view as she dug through the glove box, found the registration, then peered out cautiously as he climbed into his car.

Where to now? she wondered as she watched him start his car and pull away from the curb.

"What information would you like?" she asked her friend, then read what Marias asked for from the registration form as she waited for two cars to go by, then followed Cordell Winchester.

"Two brothers apparently," Marias said into the phone. "Same birth dates?"

"Identical twins."

"Really? Handsome?"

"As sin."

"This is a professional request, right?"

"Strictly business," Raine said and winced as she remembered the way her fist had connected with his nose. "No love lost between us."

"Oh, so that means you've 'met,'" her friend said with a laugh. "I hope it was romantic."

"If romance is him holding me down in the middle of a queen-size bed."

"Sounds good to me," Marias quipped. "Hell, sounds damned good now that I think about it. Hmm, that's interesting."

"Are you going to tell *me?*" Raine asked as she tried to keep Cordell's rental car in sight.

"I just did a little familial search. Father's name Brand. Mother a Karla Rose French. Divorced. Grandfather Call Winchester, deceased. Grandmother Pepper Winchester, still living. Got to be a nickname, wouldn't you think?"

"That's what you thought was interesting?"

"No, it's the part where Pepper Winchester's address is Whitehorse, Montana."

Cyrus and Cordell Winchester's grandmother lived here? Pepper Winchester. "Why does that name sound so familiar?" Raine said more to herself than Marias. Up the street, Cordell Winchester made a quick turn at the corner two blocks ahead of her. He'd tagged her. "Gotta go."

CORDELL COULDN'T BELIEVE it. He'd glanced in his rearview mirror and seen his brother's pickup a dozen car lengths behind him. The woman was following *him?!*

He made a quick turn, then another down an alley. Unfortunately, he met a delivery truck coming in and had to back up and take another street.

Around the next corner…

No sign of the pickup.

Cursing under his breath, he searched each side street. She couldn't have gotten away that quickly. No way.

Then he got lucky. Down a side street he spotted his brother's truck go past a few blocks away. She was headed out of town!

Unfortunately, he had a stop sign, then several cars pulled out that he had to wait for. But the second he'd gotten the chance, he'd gone after her, not surprised to see the pickup hightailing it out on one of the secondary roads south.

He had to floor the rental car to keep the pickup in sight. Cyrus would have had a heart attack if he saw the way this woman was driving his truck. The thought brought a stab of pain.

The pavement ran out. Dust boiled up behind the truck. She took a curve, throwing up gravel from the tires. Cordell backed off a little after getting the windshield of the rental car pelted, several bits of gravel pitting the glass.

He fished out his cell phone to call the sheriff's department, but found there was no cell phone service. It was just as well. At least now he could say he'd tried to call. The truth was he wanted to talk to Raine Chandler alone. He didn't want her pleading the Fifth and getting locked away behind bars where he couldn't get the truth out of her.

The narrow dirt road wound south over the rolling prairie, a roller coaster ride at this speed. He just prayed they didn't meet another vehicle coming up the road. There was barely enough room for one car. Going this fast, Raine would never be able to get far enough over to let another car pass.

At first he was convinced he would come up over a hill and find Cyrus's pickup wrecked at the bottom. But this apparently wasn't her first time driving on roads like these. He wondered what part of California she was from that she'd learned to drive on narrow dirt roads rutted with washboard.

He gave her a little space, confident that with all the dust she was throwing up, she wouldn't be able to lose him.

They left Whitehorse long behind them. As the country began to get more rugged, he realized they must be nearing the Missouri Breaks. He'd driven through the Breaks on the way to Whitehorse, crossing the Missouri River as it cut a deep gorge through this desolate, isolated country.

The country was familiar, too familiar, since he'd spent his first seven years living out here in the middle of nowhere on the Winchester Ranch. Unless he was mistaken, they weren't that far from the ranch.

Cordell was beginning to worry he'd never be able to catch her if she cut across to Highway 191. But then he saw the pickup fly over a cattle guard and come down hard, the right rear wheel hitting loose gravel on the edge of the road. He got on his brakes to keep from going airborne off the cattle guard, as well, and saw the rear of the truck fishtailing.

He could see her fighting to regain control. She almost pulled it off. Then she hit a stretch of deep washboard. The pickup tires lost traction and the next thing Cordell knew the truck was headed for the ditch adjacent to the road.

Fortunately, the ditch wasn't deep, but it was filled with water and mud which streamed up and over the truck before the vehicle finally came to a stop bogged down in the gumbo. Raine Chandler wasn't going anywhere.

Cordell was already out of his car and running toward the pickup before the driver's-side door swung open. He grabbed her and dragged her out, this time not giving her chance to go for her weapon.

Taking the gun from her jacket pocket, he stuck her pistol barrel against her temple, forcing her to her knees in the dirt next to the ditch as he held both wrists behind her. "Who put my brother in the hospital?"

"I told you—"

"I swear I will drown you in that ditch if you don't start telling me the truth."

He heard her take a deep breath and let it out slowly. She was shaking, no doubt from the adrenaline of the chase—certainly not from fear of him. There was a determination in her eyes that he'd misjudged before. He wouldn't make that mistake again.

"If you let me up, I'll tell you everything."

He let out a bark of a laugh. "You think I'm going to fall for that again?"

"I already told you. I was crossing the parking lot behind the hotel when someone tried to run me down. Your brother shoved me out of the way, I fell and that's all I remember. I must have blacked out for a moment because when I came to, your brother was lying there on the ground and I could hear sirens."

He pushed her down harder, pressing the gun barrel into her temple. "Why didn't you stay and tell the sheriff's deputy what had happened?"

She shook her head, making him want to throttle her. "I told you. I was scared. I panicked."

"Bull. You didn't want to be involved. Why?"

"I was scared."

He couldn't imagine anything scaring this woman. He also didn't believe she'd come back to the hotel this morning to find out Cyrus's name. So what had she been looking for?

"Do you have a permit to carry this gun?"

She hesitated a little too long. "Not in Montana."

"Why are you carrying a gun anyway?" he demanded.

"I live in L.A. You'd carry a gun, too."

Cordell didn't know what to think. Was it possible Cyrus had just been in the wrong place at the wrong time? Or was this woman lying through her teeth?

"Why would someone want to run you down?"

"How would I know? Maybe they mistook me for someone else. Or maybe it was an accident. Now would you please let me up?"

"Like your tire on your car just happened to be slashed?"

He sighed. He was getting nowhere with her. He let go of her hands, standing back in case she came up fighting, which he half expected. To his surprise, she got slowly to her feet.

"How is your brother?" she asked quietly.

"He's in a coma." Cordell had to look away. Just saying the words made it all too real.

"I'm sorry." She sounded surprised and sympathetic.

"Good," he said. "Because you're going to help me find the person who did this to him."

"I told you I don't know who was behind the wheel of that van."

That, he thought, might actually be the truth. But he suspected she knew damned well why the person had cut her tire and then tried to run her down. Cyrus couldn't have gotten downstairs from the fourth floor fast enough, unless he'd seen the man knife her tire and then go wait for her in the van with the motor running.

Cordell stepped to the open door of the pickup and took out her purse, an overnight bag with a small laptop computer tucked in the side and a large leather satchel. Laying each in the grass, he began to go through them, keeping the gun within reach should he need it.

"Please, that's my personal—"

"Stay right where you are," he warned her.

She stopped moving toward him, looking resigned as he opened her purse and quickly searched it. A little over two hundred in cash, most in crisp new twenties probably straight from the ATM machine. A California driver's license. He glanced at the information on it. Twenty-six.

Nothing unusual in her overnight bag.

He was beginning to wonder if she might really be telling the truth when he opened the large leather satchel. *"What the hell?"*

Chapter Four

Raine was still reeling from what he'd told her. His brother was in a coma? She felt sick to her stomach even before Cordell opened her satchel.

"I asked you what the hell this is," he demanded, taking a step toward her, shock and disbelief contorting his handsome face.

"I'm a journalist." The lie didn't come easily even though it was the one she'd been using for her cover. She hated lying to him. She'd inadvertently gotten his brother into this. She felt guilty enough. Lying didn't make it any easier. But she still couldn't be sure she could trust this man....

"A *journalist?*" Cordell grimaced as he glanced again at the photographs in the satchel. "This is about some *article?*"

"Are you going to question everything I say to you?" she demanded, going on the offensive.

"I am until I hear something I can believe."

She tried a little truth on him. "I'm working on an old missing person's case, a child who was abducted sixteen years ago from Whitehorse. Her name was Emily Frank."

Cordell studied her openly before pulling out the stack of photographs from the abductions. As many times as she had looked at the photos, she never failed to be moved to tears by the piles of charred bones, the rusted fifty-five-gallon barrels where the remains were found or the faces of the children still missing—and presumed dead.

Cordell shoved back his Stetson, looking shaken and uncertain, as he pulled out all the research material she'd gathered. "All *this* is related to the article you're working on?" he asked in disbelief.

She nodded.

"This child, Emily Frank... Tell me you aren't here looking for her remains."

"No. I'm interviewing the people who knew her."

He was watching her closely as if he knew she was leaving out some key piece of information—and wondering why. "So how many people have you interviewed?"

She knew where he was headed with this. He was trying to decide if her article research was connected to his brother's accident.

"None. I only got to the town yesterday," she said. "I haven't had a chance to talk to anyone yet."

He frowned. "Someone knows you're in town."

He was right about that, she thought and added truthfully, "I have no idea how they might have found out."

Cordell sighed. "What newspaper or magazine do you work for?"

She tried not to glance away from his black bottomless gaze. "I'm freelancing this one."

"How about a home address, a former newspaper or magazine, someone who can verify your story."

She felt her eyes narrow as she met his gaze. "My mother took off when I was a baby. I never knew my father. I've been on my own since I was eighteen. I put all my things into storage before I left California. I wasn't sure how long I'd be gone. So, no, I don't have a home address or anyone who can verify what I'm working on."

"*Someone* knows," he snapped and pulled off his Stetson to rake his fingers through his hair. "Chucking it all for a story, that's some dedication to your work. Why Montana? I'm sure there are missing children in California. There must be hundreds of stories you could have done there, if not thousands. Why this particular case?"

She was forced to look away. "I saw a picture of her. There was just something in her eyes…" She swallowed back the lump in her throat.

"I'm going to have to go through all of your notes, everything you have on this case."

She balked, just as she was sure he'd known she would.

"I should mention," he said, his words like thrown stones, "I went to the sheriff this morning. She just happens to be my cousin. I told her you stole my brother's pickup and might have been involved in the attack on him. She's already put an APB out on you because you left the scene. Unless you want to go to jail, I suggest you reconsider."

"I've told you what *I'm* doing here," she said, shaken to hear that his cousin was sheriff. "Why don't you tell me what brings two private investigators to Whitehorse, Montana?"

His eyebrows shot up. He hadn't expected her to find out who he was. Along with surprise though, there was grudging admiration in his gaze. "Not that it's any of your business but my brother and I came here to see our grandmother, Pepper Winchester. She's…dying."

She flinched as a shaft of guilt pierced her conscience. She believed him. Just as she believed his shocked reaction to the photographs in her satchel. This man wasn't working for a sexual child predator. At least she hoped not.

"Come on, we need to go somewhere so I can go through all of this," he said. "Or are you going to lie to me and tell me that all of this doesn't have something to do with you and the article you're writing?"

She wasn't.

He nodded, seeming relieved for once she wasn't going to argue the point. "Since my brother's pickup isn't going anywhere until a wrecker pulls it out, you're riding with me."

"I'd like to speak to the nurse at the hospital first," she said.

He turned back to look at her.

"I just want to verify what you've told me about your brother."

"I've heard that journalists don't take anyone's word on anything without at least a backup source, but do you really think I'd lie about my brother being in a coma?" Even under the shade of his cowboy hat, she could see the piercing black of his gaze. He was angry and she really couldn't blame him.

He shook his head in obvious disgust. "Fine. When we get to a place where my phone works, you're welcome to call the hospital." He swore under his breath. "Are you always this paranoid?"

"Only when people really are after me."

He sighed and pulled out his cell phone. "No coverage. Or do you want to check yourself?"

"I'll take your word for it until cell phone service is available."

He shook his head. "That's real damned big of you. Let me make something clear, I'm not sure what happened last night but I have a pretty good idea. You and your article got my brother into this. If guilt or the threat of jail doesn't work, then I'll use whatever methods I have to, but you *will* help me find the people who did this to him, one way or another."

CORDELL COULDN'T believe this mess. Cyrus in a coma and him saddled with this journalist and her paranoia.

Now what the hell was he going to do with her? he asked himself as he studied Raine Chandler. The cool breeze stirred the hair at the nape of his neck and he turned to see a dark bank of clouds on the horizon to the west. Great, just what he needed. A thunderstorm and him miles from a paved road.

He remembered as a kid how the roads would be impassable until after a storm when the wind and sun dried things out.

He considered making a run for town, but he could tell by the way the clouds were moving in that he would never make it before the storm hit. The rental car would be worthless and his brother's pickup was buried in the mud and not going anywhere. He swore under his breath again.

There was only one place to go.

As much as he hated it, he knew it was the best plan given the storm and the fact that he needed to take Raine somewhere so he could go through all of her research materials. His brother might have stumbled onto trouble last night, but Raine Chandler was up to her neck in it.

All he had to do was find the people after her.

That meant going to a private spot where she didn't try to get away from him until he found out what he needed. Cordell groaned at the thought though. "Come on."

"Where are we going?"

"To my grandmother's ranch. It's closer than town." He saw something flicker in her eyes. "Or would you rather go to jail?"

"Maybe I'd be safer there."

He stopped to give her his full attention. "If you think

your virtue might be at risk coming with me, then let me set you straight. You aren't my type and I have much more important things on my mind than sex. That blunt enough for you?"

"Quite. Did I mention that I believe Emily Frank was taken by someone in one of Whitehorse's more prominent seemingly upstanding families?"

Cordell let out a hoot of laughter. "Like the *Winchesters?* Think again. We've never been upstanding. Not even seemingly."

"You might be surprised how money and power tip the scales toward upstanding."

"No, actually I wouldn't be surprised." He eyed her, realizing she'd researched his family. Before or after Cyrus had crossed her path? "Winchester is just a name to me. I haven't been back here in twenty-seven years and if there were any money or power, my father and brother and I have never been a part of it."

She cocked a brow at him. "What about your grandmother?"

"Not that it is any of your business, but until recently my grandmother was a recluse who hadn't left the ranch in all those years. None of the rest of us had seen her in all that time or lived anywhere near here. Even if she hadn't been locked away for twenty-seven years, I can assure you she wouldn't abduct a child."

"If you haven't seen her, then you have no way of knowing—"

"My grandmother," he interrupted, "is so fond of children she doesn't even know how many grandchildren she has. She had to pay her lawyer to try to track us all down. I won't even go into how she treated her own children, even her favorite son."

"And this is where you're taking me? To see this grandmother?" She sounded incredulous.

"It wouldn't be my first choice, but you've left us no other option." Thunder rumbled in the distance. "You know anything about storms up in this country? Unless we get moving and damned soon, that storm is going to catch us and we are going to be stuck, literally, out here until someone comes along and that could be a damned long time. Once it starts raining, this road will become gumbo. We'd never be able to get back to town before the storm hits so we're going to wait out the storm at the Winchester Ranch. And believe me, I'm much unhappier about that prospect than you could ever be."

What in her research was she trying so desperately to keep from him? he wondered. Well, he'd soon find out. Once they reached the ranch, he'd go through everything in that satchel. She was his only possible connection to the men who'd put his brother in a coma. She was going to help him even if he had to wring her pretty little neck.

It would make it easier if she trusted him though, but he didn't take it personally. If he'd learned anything from his first marriage and subsequent divorce, it was that trust is a fragile thing that once broken badly is impossible to get back again.

He wondered, though, who had broken Raine Chandler's trust. Whoever it was had done a bang-up job.

Raine realized she had little choice but to go with him to the Winchester Ranch. Fighting Cordell would be futile since right now he held all the cards.

Also she wanted the man who'd hurt his brother just as badly as he did. If it was true and Cyrus Winchester was now fighting for his life, she owed him for his chivalry in saving her last night.

Cordell Winchester was another story. He didn't have a chivalrous bone in his body and she balked at being forced into anything, especially by him.

But she also realized it couldn't hurt having an obviously high-priced private investigator now helping her find the person who'd been driving that van last night—the same person she'd come to Whitehorse to find.

As she started to gather up her things he'd dumped in the grass, Cordell stopped her. "I'll take care of this."

"I'd prefer to carry my own things."

He smiled. "I'd prefer you not bloody my nose or kick me in the groin or pull a gun on me."

"That's right, you have my gun. I'd like that back."

"I'm sure you would. But you don't need to worry. From now until we're finished with this, I will keep you safe."

She lifted a brow questioning whether he thought he really could handle that job. Fortunately she'd learned to take care of herself. "I'm not sure you won't need my help."

He gave her a look that said she was pushing her luck. She heard him swear under his breath as he walked away. She watched him, trying to gauge what kind of man he really was. One thing was for sure—he had no idea who the woman he'd just taken captive really was.

As she watched him, for the first time, she took a good look at Cordell Winchester. She was suddenly aware of the man on some primitive level. He looked like an ad for Montana, a cowboy who was just as comfortable in the wild outdoors as in a large city or a boardroom.

She must have been blind not to have noticed before this how his jeans hugged his tight behind, the legs long, the hips slim. His shoulders seemed broad enough to block out the sun.

Raine felt desire warm her blood. It had been a long time since she'd been even remotely aware of a man. She'd been too busy with her career. She'd apparently forgotten what it felt like to want a man so much it made her ache. Or maybe she'd just never known a man like Cordell Winchester, a man who could unleash that kind of primal need even when she couldn't stand the sight of him.

This was a man who had to be used to getting what he wanted from women. She was glad she wasn't that type of woman. But the thought also came with a little regret that she wouldn't be finding out if Cordell was as sexy as he looked.

As he started to the car with her things, he saw her eyeing him. "Something wrong?"

She scoffed at that. Everything was wrong. She couldn't wait to see the last of this Winchester and, judging by the expression on Cordell's face, he felt the same way.

CORDELL HATED THE IDEA of dragging this woman out to the ranch with him as much as he hated going there in the first place. He knew he had no business taking her prisoner and the last person he wanted to see was his grandmother.

But the storm had given him no other option other than being trapped in the small rental car with her. That, he thought, could definitely be worse than the ranch. At least at his grandmother's they should be able to get something to eat and drink and, if they were stuck there overnight, a place to sleep.

He didn't trust Raine Chandler as far as he could toss her and needed this time to find out everything he could about her—and this article she was writing.

As it was, he'd have to watch her 24/7. At least at the ranch, she was far enough from Whitehorse that taking off would require she hoof it forty miles. Or take a horse. He couldn't see that happening.

"This is just temporary," he said as they climbed into the car. Once he found the person who hurt his brother, Raine Chandler was free to do whatever the hell she wanted.

"So," he said and started the car, "why don't you tell me about this article you're working on."

She sighed. "Her name, as I already told you, was

Emily Frank. She was ten when she was taken as she walked home from school. She was never found. Neither were her abductors."

He shot her a surprised look. "You said abductors? Are you saying there was more than one person who took her?"

"A man and a woman."

"How do you know that?"

She seemed to hesitate. "I have something of the girl's."

He felt a chill trot the length of his spine. "It's just hard to imagine a woman—"

"Sometimes a woman in these situations is more dangerous than the man. She often goes along with it to make him happy but resents it—and is hateful to the child because she is jealous. In a few cases, it is her idea."

Cordell gripped the steering wheel tighter as he drove, sickened by the things she was telling him. "These people are monsters."

"A common misconception is that they are recognizable psychos," she said, as if warming to her subject. "Look at the famous cases. The neighbors always say, 'They seemed like such a normal family.' They hide behind the facade of being upstanding citizens. Often they are very involved in their community, do a lot of good deeds and are high profile. Money and power masquerading as the wholesome family next door. They're people you could pass on the street and never suspect. These people appear so normal that the good people of Whitehorse have no idea that these child abductors live right among them."

CORDELL LOOKED SHOCKED and sick to his stomach. She saw him grip the steering wheel tighter.

"You said Emily was taken sixteen years ago," he said after a long moment.

She knew what he was asking. "Who knows how many more children they have taken since that time."

"Come on, residents would become suspicious if a bunch of kids went missing from a small Montana town."

Raine shook her head. "These people are serial child abductors. They don't stop. They don't have to. They're bulletproof because they're so deeply rooted in the community and the children they take are on the remote edge of society."

He frowned over at her.

"Children from families with few resources or connections to the town. Foster children."

"These children are still going to be reported missing."

"Missing and presumed runaways. Because of that the foster parents often don't alert the authorities right away. Even when they do and the child isn't found, the victim is considered a runaway until her body is found."

Cordell didn't say anything for a long time. "Isn't that going to make the abductors nearly impossible to find?"

"That's why they haven't been caught. These people

will do anything to keep their twisted secret." She felt his gaze on her.

"Including making another run at you?"

Cordell Winchester was smart. She liked how quickly he'd understood the situation.

She started to argue that the hit-and-run last night had nothing to do with her—or her reason for being in Whitehorse. She saved her breath. "They'll send someone after me again," she said simply.

If they haven't already, she thought, studying the cowboy sitting next to her. "That is, if they can find me at some isolated ranch in the middle of nowhere."

He chuckled as the car sped down the narrow dirt road. "We're just sitting out the storm at my grandmother's. Don't worry, I'll make sure you can use yourself as bait if that's your plan."

"What a relief." Raine stared out at the rolling prairie. He'd also been right about the storm. It moved in quickly, the first drops of rain splattering against the windshield. Ahead the land seemed to break up into badlands and she knew they must be nearing the Missouri Breaks. On her way to Whitehorse, she'd dropped down into the Breaks to cross the winding river as it made its way through Montana.

She'd never seen such wild, isolated country. Now she realized just how far they were from civilization. Normally, she felt she could hold her own. But Cordell Winchester outweighed her and was obviously much stronger. He also had her gun. And now a storm had blown in, one that he swore could strand them out here.

So why wasn't she terrified? She glanced over at him, studying his expression and seeing nothing but pain. She could see that he was worried sick about his brother. And he'd been visibly shaken by the photographs of the abducted children.

Was it possible he was in town just to see his grandmother, and his brother had just been in the wrong place at the wrong time last night? It was beginning to seem that way.

She studied him, realizing he was much harder to read than most people. He must make a damned good private investigator. And like her, she suspected he didn't let most people in.

There was something about him that made her also suspect he'd been hurt by someone. She felt that, rather than saw it, a built-in empathy for others you recognize because they've gone through something akin to what you have. A sixth sense. Who had hurt him? she wondered.

Raine heard Cordell swear as rain pinged off the hood, falling harder and faster. The car swerved several times in the mud forming on the surface of the road. Ahead she spotted a huge log arch over a narrow, weed-choked road. The sign on the arch read, Winchester Ranch, and Cordell seemed to relax as he slowed the car to make the turn.

She felt her heart beat a little faster as he drove down the road, the weeds between the ruts scraping loudly along the undercarriage to the beat of the pouring rain. She could feel the tires spinning out as the ranch lodge came into view.

Out of the corner of her eye, she saw that Cordell's expression was one of dread. "So you really haven't been here in twenty-seven years?"

"Not since I was seven. This is the first time I've been invited back."

"You must have been a pretty awful kid."

Through the rain and the sweep of the wipers, she stared at the ranch buildings nestled against the hillside. The place looked very Western and rustic. A sprawling log structure, it ran out in at least a couple of wings and climbed to three stories on one of what appeared to be an older wing.

"About my grandmother... She's..." He seemed at a loss for words. He let out a sigh. "You'll see soon enough."

Raine sat up straighter as they dropped down the slippery slope to the massive ranch lodge, not surprised that she was anxious to meet Cordell's grandmother.

"How do you plan to explain me?" she asked.

He gave a devastating smile that made the interior of the car seem too intimate and definitely too close. "I'm going to tell her you're a car thief."

"That should impress her," she said as he brought the car to a stop in front of the log mammoth. A curtain moved on the second floor. An old blue heeler hobbled out into the rain to growl next to the car. Other than that, nothing moved.

"Didn't I hear something about a couple of murders on this ranch a month or so ago?" Raine asked as it suddenly hit her why the name Pepper Winchester had sounded so familiar.

Chapter Five

"I'm sure it won't be the last murder out here, either," Cordell said as he stared at the ranch lodge. If it hadn't been for the rain, he would have turned around and left. But the roads had already begun to turn to gumbo.

Now he would have to see his grandmother when he hadn't been the one who'd wanted to come here in the first place. Cyrus had been the one determined to see this place and now— Just the thought of his brother brought a wave of pain. The twin connection that had comforted him since they were born was still gone. He felt as if a part of him had been ripped out.

He'd left his number with the hospital along with instructions that they were to call if there was any change at all in his twin's condition. Unfortunately, there was no cell phone service out here. He checked his phone anyway. No messages. He didn't know whether to feel relieved or more concerned. He just had to believe that Cyrus would come out of this.

"Looks like we'll have to make a run for it," he said, noting that the rain didn't look as if it planned to let up.

As he got out of the car, Cordell realized it had probably

been a mistake to bring Raine here. Next thing he knew she'd be doing an investigative piece on the Winchesters and who knew how many more secrets were hidden in these old walls?

The front door opened as he and Raine ran toward the lodge. He was taken aback to realize the small, broomstick-thin elderly woman in the doorway was Enid Hoagland. His brother Cyrus would have gotten a kick out of the fact that the mean old woman was still alive.

"Which one are you?" Enid demanded as she stepped back to let them into the small foyer.

Before he could answer, his grandmother appeared. "He's Cordell," Pepper Winchester said. "Enid, why don't you make something hot to drink for our guests? They're soaked to the skin."

Enid didn't look the least bit happy about being sent away. For a moment, Cordell thought she would refuse to go. But with a huff, she turned and disappeared into the dim interior.

He was shocked that his grandmother had recognized him. She hadn't been able to tell him and Cyrus apart when they were younger. Why now? Unless maybe she'd heard about Cyrus's accident.

"This must be your wife," Pepper said, turning her gaze on Raine.

Cordell flushed, realizing of course his grandmother hadn't heard about his divorce. He'd just assumed everyone for thousands of miles around would have heard since it had been such an ugly one.

"No, this is Raine Chandler," he said. "My wife and I are divorced."

His grandmother raised a brow. "So like my attorney to get it wrong. I'd fire him if he was still in my employ." She smiled as she shook Raine's hand, her old eyes seeming to bore into the younger woman.

"Raine is an investigative reporter," he said.

Pepper winced.

"Don't worry, she isn't investigating the Winchesters." He took a breath and let it out slowly. "At least not yet," he said under his breath. "So you've heard. Cyrus was attacked last night outside his hotel room in Whitehorse and is in the hospital in a coma."

Pepper's hands went to her chest. "I hadn't heard. Is he…"

His grandmother's concern surprised him. That and the fact that she really had been able to distinguish him from his brother apparently. Had she always been and just hadn't bothered?

"It's too early to know his prognosis," Cordell said. "The doctor is hopeful he will regain consciousness soon. We all are."

"Yes," his grandmother agreed. "I'm sorry." She glanced out at the rental car. "You'll have to bring in your own bags. Alfred…"

"Yes, I heard. But we won't be staying," Cordell said.

"Why ever not?" his grandmother demanded.

"We're just here to wait out the storm," he said.

She raised a brow. "You were just in the area and

decided to drop by? Enid has already made up two rooms anyway."

Cordell started to argue, but realized this might be for the best. He and Raine would have the privacy they needed if they had rooms away from his grandmother and Enid. And if the storm let up...

"So this investigative piece you're writing..." Pepper said, turning to Raine now that the lodging was settled.

"It's about child abductions, one in particular. You might remember it. A ten-year-old girl named Emily Frank. She was abducted on her way home from school sixteen years ago in Whitehorse."

Pepper frowned. "I'm sorry, I *don't* remember." But clearly she also didn't want to hear any more about it. "I'll make sure Enid has your rooms ready while Cordell gets your bags." With that she turned and left them.

THE PHONE RANG AS Pepper Winchester started down the hall. She picked up one of the extensions before Enid could. "Hello."

The news about Cordell's twin had shaken her. But given the information, she wasn't surprised to hear the voice on the other end of the line.

"Mother?" She hadn't heard her son Brand Winchester's voice in twenty-seven years. It surprised her that it could fill her with such a landslide of emotions. "Have you heard about Cyrus?"

"Yes, just now when Cordell arrived. He's out bringing in his bags."

"He's staying there?" He sounded both surprised and disapproving.

"Don't worry, there hasn't been a murder here in weeks," Pepper said, unable to contain her annoyance.

"I heard about that. I'm going to be coming out."

Her daughter, Virginia, had said it would take a gun to Brand's head to get him to ever come back to the ranch even for a visit. Pepper couldn't wait to tell Virginia how wrong she'd been. It had taken his son's accident to get Brand back here.

"I hope you'll stay here at the ranch." She didn't mention that his old-maid sister Virginia was also here. She didn't think Virginia's presence at the ranch would be a draw for her brother, but just the opposite.

Brand hesitated so long Pepper found herself getting irritated and had to squelch saying something she would regret.

"All right," he finally agreed and Pepper heard the telltale sound of Enid replacing the extension in the kitchen. "I'll be there tomorrow after I see Cyrus at the hospital."

"Plan on having supper with us," Pepper said. "The roads should be dry enough by then." She hung up and stood for moment thinking that her plan had worked in ways she hadn't expected.

After twenty-seven years, they were all wandering back to the ranch. She found little satisfaction in it, though, as she walked down the hall and shoved open the kitchen door. She'd thought that letting them believe she was dying would do the trick—that and greed. Surprisingly only one had fallen for that—Virginia.

Pepper shoved her annoyance with her only daughter away and considered that things might work out after all. With luck she would discover which of her spawn was a traitor and a murderer.

"MY GRANDMOTHER WASN'T being insensitive about the story you're working on. Although she *can* be insensitive without much effort," Cordell said, seeing Raine's expression when he returned with the bags from the car.

He shook off the rain from his jacket as he set down the bags in the entryway. She hadn't packed much for a possible extended stay in Montana. He wondered how long she'd planned to stay.

"As I told you, my grandmother's been a recluse for the past twenty-seven years," he continued when she didn't say anything. "I'm sure she didn't hear about anything that's happened during that time."

"What made her become a recluse?" Raine asked, looking into the dim interior of the house beyond the entryway.

"Her youngest son had disappeared, believed to have run off," he said, keeping his voice down. "Apparently it was more than she could bear." Cordell hesitated as a thought struck him. "Funny, but she seems to be taking his murder better than his disappearance. Odd, huh."

"He was *murdered?*"

Cordell nodded. "Twenty-seven years ago. So what do you think she did? She invited the rest of her family back to Winchester Ranch, a family she hadn't seen in all those years."

"Maybe she wants to try to make up for it before she dies."

He shook his head. "She's up to something, something no good."

"But you still came back."

"I only came back because of my brother Cyrus. You and I are here only because of the storm and I needed someplace where I can keep an eye on you."

"You're not very trusting, are you?"

He didn't bother to answer. "You couldn't get me within five hundred miles of this place and that old woman in there if I had any other choice." He saw Raine's reaction. "Do you believe in evil?"

She seemed startled by the question.

"I don't know if it is this place or what this place does to people."

"Places aren't evil. People are," she said with conviction.

"Are you going to spend the rest of the day out there talking or let me show you to your rooms?" Enid demanded as she suddenly appeared, startling them both.

"Speaking of evil," Cordell said under his breath.

RAINE LOOKED AROUND the ranch lodge, wondering about the Winchesters, especially Cordell Winchester, as she followed Enid up the stairs.

Divorced. She should have known. That could explain

the coldness she'd felt in him. His ex had broken his heart, she'd bet money on it. He had all the classic symptoms of a man who had been betrayed by the woman he'd loved.

She dragged her gaze away from him and considered his weird family and this place where they lived that he thought evil. The Winchester Ranch lodge looked as if it had been dropped from an old Western movie set. The log walls, a rich patina, were covered with Native American rugs, dead animal heads and Western art that looked old and expensive.

Enid was faster than she looked and Raine had to hurry to catch her, Cordell coming slowly up the stairs behind them.

Enid opened a door into a large room with a sitting room and huge bed and private bath. "This is your room," she said as if she thought Raine planned to sneak off and find Cordell's as soon as the lights went out. "Cordell's room is across the hall." Enid glanced down the stairs as if to make it known that anyone on the lower floor would be able to see her if she left her room for any reason.

"Thank you," Raine said, wishing she was in some nondescript motel room. She'd never liked staying with strangers and the Winchester family and the hired help seemed about as strange as anyone could get.

As she glanced at Cordell, she was reminded of his brother. She could see the worry on his face and felt overwhelmed with guilt at the knowledge that the twin brother who'd saved her life was now fighting for his. She had no choice but to help Cordell.

"Your room is across the hall," Enid said to Cordell.

"Thank you," he said. "That will be all."

The elderly housekeeper gave him a withering look, spun on her heel and disappeared down the staircase.

Cordell stepped through the open door to his equally large suitelike room and set down Raine's overnight bag, purse and satchel on the table. He glanced at the fire going in the fireplace, then at the open-curtained French doors that led out onto the small balcony.

"I'm not going to try to escape," Raine said, entering his room. "I'd like my things in my room."

He nodded toward her overnight bag and purse. "They're all yours. I still need to go through the satchel."

Her gaze went to the double bed on the ornate iron frame. It was identical to the one in her room and would take a footstool to climb into it. Several homemade quilts were piled onto the end of the bed, making her wonder how cold it got out here at night.

Enid had made a point of letting them know she thought they were already sleeping together and that being forced to get two rooms ready only made more work for her. The old woman wasn't as sharp as she thought she was, Raine thought. But the grandmother... well, Raine thought everyone probably underestimated her.

Cordell dumped the contents of her leather satchel

onto the table by the window and Raine closed the bedroom door behind her. She didn't want him going through everything without her here. Nor did she want everyone in the household to know what they would be discussing. Cordell didn't seem to notice she hadn't left.

She liked the sound of the rain as she stepped to the French doors, opening them a crack. She felt as if she needed the fresh air. She'd never liked being closed in. She looked out over the ranch, feeling antsy and wondering how long they would have to stay here. There was something about the place that made her uneasy. Or was she just anxious about what was going to happen next?

"Hopefully the rain will stop soon and it will dry up enough that we will be able to leave later tonight," Cordell said behind her.

Raine watched the pouring rain thinking his grandmother was probably right. They were stranded here at least for the night.

She closed the door and stepped back into the room. Cordell had sat down at the table and was gingerly looking through the photographs and other information she'd gathered. She took a chair across from him.

"If you're just writing about Emily Frank, why do you have all these other photographs of missing children?" he asked.

She could tell the faces of all those missing children were taking their toll on him. It was impossible to look into all that innocence and know horrible things had been done to those children before their bodies had been dumped or buried or, in the case of the people Raine was looking for, burned like trash when they were finished with them.

"Because this isn't just about Emily," she said. "There are serial child abductors out there. Some keep the children a short period of time and kill them. Others keep them until the child is too old, then they get rid of that one and get another one the right age."

Cordell swore under his breath. "These statistics can't be right. About eight hundred thousand children are reported missing every year or two thousand a day?"

"Over fifty thousand of those are victims of abductions by strangers. The others are taken by family members or people they know."

"I had no idea," he said, clearly upset.

"Few people do unless it hits closer to home for them. Almost all of the ones abducted by strangers are taken by men."

"I don't understand how this can happen."

"In eighty percent of the abductions by strangers, the first contact occurs within a quarter mile of the child's home. In many cases, so does the abduction. Most strangers grab their victims on the street or try to lure them into their vehicles. About seventy-four percent of the victims are girls."

Patiently, she stood and picked up a map. Opening it, she spread the map of Montana out on the table and saw his eyes widen when he noticed the dozens of colored stars.

"Don't tell me that is where children have gone missing," he said.

"The blues ones are believed to be runaways. The yellow ones are considered solved cases based either on a suspect's confession or the discovery of remains. The red ones are unsolved missing children cases."

He stared down at the map, a look of horror on his face. "And the green stars?"

"Those are only the cases a man named Orville Cline confessed to in this state. In only one study, child molesters averaged over a hundred child victims per molester."

Cordell pushed back his chair and walked over to the fireplace. She watched him grab the mantel and lower his head. "This Orville Cline, where is he now?"

"Serving time at Montana State Prison in Deer Lodge. He confessed to taking Emily Frank and killing her."

Cordell spun around in surprise. "Wait, if—"

"He lied. I have evidence that he couldn't possibly have taken Emily Frank." She picked up the folder on Orville Cline and handed it to Cordell, who read it standing up. She watched him read the confessions Orville had made during the trial. Raine had read this so many times, she could have recited the man's confession to Emily Frank's abduction and murder verbatim.

Cordell snapped the folder shut and looked up in surprise. "Why would he confess in horrific detail about an abduction and murder he'd didn't commit? Maybe he confused her with another little girl."

Raine shook her head. "They don't forget or mix up

their victims. That's part of the high they get out of it, remembering. He knew he didn't take Emily Frank."

"Then why confess?"

She rose and walked over to the French doors again. The rain had stopped and now a cool breeze swept across the balcony smelling sweet and summery. "I think he made some kind of deal with the couple who really abducted Emily."

"But you don't know that for a fact."

"No, but I do know that he lied about it," she said, turning back to him. "Open the small manila envelope." She opened the door wider. The breeze felt soothing against her cheek as she listened to him sort through the items on the desk. She heard him open it, heard his sharp intake of breath, then the silence that followed broken only by the rustle of the sixteen-year-old spiral notebook pages.

"My God," Cordell said behind her. "Emily wrote this?"

"She kept a diary of the days she was imprisoned after her abduction. Her handwritten notes contradict what Orville Cline said happened. He lied."

Cordell frowned. "Where did you get these?"

"They were sent to me recently."

That surprised him.

"I don't know from whom or what their motive is, but I believe they want me to find out the truth about Emily Frank's abduction."

"Orville Cline?"

"Doubtful. I think it was one of the people who abducted Emily."

"Why would… Are you telling me you think one of them wants the truth to come out?"

She shrugged. "That's what I thought until someone tried to run me down last night."

"Exactly. It looks more like they just tricked you into coming up here. If you're telling the truth, someone tried to kill you last night. That was no accident behind the hotel." He was frowning again. "But why? If Orville Cline confessed to Emily Frank's killing, they are in the clear. So…why contact *you?*"

"Journalists are often targets," she hedged. "Especially ones who might have some new information on the case."

"Can you prove this Orville Cline couldn't have taken Emily?"

"Not yet," she admitted. "But that diary Emily kept proves he lied about the details."

Cordell looked down at the pages with the heartbreaking words neatly printed on them. Like her, he had to be awed by the girl's courage, her hope and faith in a world that hadn't been kind to her, her perseverance in such a horrible situation. Emily believed she would be rescued.

"The person who sent you these has to be involved," he said quietly as if the full weight was just now making an impact on him. "If you're right and Emily wasn't the only child they abducted and there is even a chance that this person wants the abductions to stop…"

"Now do you understand why I'm here, why I'm willing to risk my life?"

ENID HAD A SCOWL ON her face when Pepper walked into the kitchen. Nothing new there. She studied her housekeeper, considering giving her hell for eavesdropping on her private conversation. But Enid had been eavesdropping for years. It was one reason she was still employed here. She'd overheard too much.

"Brand is coming," Pepper said. "Please make a room for him. I told him to plan on having supper with us."

Enid grunted unhappily and Pepper had to wonder why the woman stayed. Then grimaced at her own foolishness. Enid was here only for one thing: the Winchester fortune. She planned to get her share. One way or another.

An uneasy truce had hung between them since the latest secrets had been uncovered at the ranch. Though no bargain was made, it was assumed that Enid would stay on at the ranch as housekeeper and cook. But she would be rewarded for her loyalty.

The elderly Enid never spoke of her husband's murder nor did she seem to grieve for his loss. If anything, Alfred appeared quickly forgotten by his wife.

Pepper understood such behavior, though she secretly believed she'd been grieving for her own lost husband for years.

"Did you see what your latest grandson dragged in here?" Enid said, raising her eyes to the ceiling where she'd made up rooms for Cordell and the young reporter. "We'll be lucky not to be murdered in our sleep."

Pepper laughed at that. She'd put money on herself and Enid being much more dangerous than that young woman upstairs. She watched Enid make a vegetable beef soup for their lunch. It had been days since the elderly cook had attempted to drug her.

For months after her son Trace's disappearance, Pepper had welcomed the drugs Enid surreptitiously slipped her. She had welcomed the oblivion. She hadn't even considered why Enid was doing it.

But once Trace's murder had come to light, everything had changed. Pepper now wanted her wits about her. She was in search of the truth about her son's murder and suspected there had been an accomplice—right in this house.

It was why she'd gotten her family back here. Also why she dumped most cups of tea her housekeeper brought her down the drain.

Enid was no fool. She had to know. Which made her wonder what Enid would do next.

One thing Pepper knew for certain. It was just a matter of time before the aging housekeeper would demand payment for keeping Pepper's secrets.

"I'm going to find Cordell," Pepper said, gripping her cane.

Enid shot her a disapproving look. "I hope you're not planning to ask another one to stay on the ranch."

"With Alfred gone, we need Jack here," she said of her grandson Jack Winchester. Jack had promised to come back. He and his new bride, Josey, were on an extended honeymoon, but Pepper was hoping when he returned that he would take her up on his offer to turn Winchester Ranch into a working ranch again.

"That new bride of his isn't going to want to come back here," Enid said.

"It can be lonely and sometimes the wind..." She shook her head, remembering how the sound of the wind had nearly driven her crazy when her husband had brought her here after their honeymoon. "It can be a harsh, unforgiving place."

Enid huffed at that. "Life is what you make it." Her gaze met Pepper's. "But I guess I don't have to tell you that. You've managed fine, haven't you?"

She heard the insinuation in Enid's words. Keeping secrets was a dangerous proposition, Pepper wanted to tell her. Enid thought she had her right where she wanted her. But Pepper had a plan.

Actually, she felt it was her duty not to leave this world without first making sure this mean, old bitch was sent straight to hell ahead of her.

Chapter Six

Cordell started at the knock and quickly put all of the documents back into Raine's satchel.

At the door he found the housekeeper. "Your grandmother wants a word with you down in the parlor," Enid said. "Also dinner will be served tonight at six sharp. Don't be late."

Cordell had been waiting for the other shoe to drop since receiving the letter from his grandmother's lawyer. He glanced back at Raine, hating to leave her alone.

"Do I have time to take a bath?" she asked, getting to her feet. When she reached to take the satchel with her to her room, he stopped her, saying, "Leave that. I'd like to look at it again. I need to go see what my grandmother wants."

She nodded and scooped up her computer. He didn't say anything, pretty sure she couldn't get Internet service out here and what difference would it make if she could?

"We'll leave as soon as we can. Believe me, I'm more anxious to get out of here than you are."

Cordell waited until Raine disappeared into her room

across the hall before he stepped out, closed and locked his own room. Enid saw him pocket the old skeleton key. He knew he'd only managed to increase her curiosity.

Pepper was waiting for him, standing at the window leaning on her cane in what Enid had called the parlor. It was a nice-size room with leather furniture, a stone fireplace and a single large window that opened to the front of the house. Even though it was June, a blaze burned in the fireplace, but did little to do away with the chill in this house.

When she heard him enter the room, Pepper turned and took one of the chairs. He sat across from her in a matching leather chair. It creaked under his weight and he realized this was the same furniture they'd had when he was a kid living here. In fact, little about the lodge had changed over the past twenty-seven years. Everything was more worn, but the memories were still fresh.

"I had hoped you would have answered my letter to let me know when you would be arriving," his grandmother said reproachfully.

"The letter wasn't from you, but your attorney, and I didn't see any reason to answer it. Truthfully, I'd hoped I could change Cyrus's mind about coming out to the ranch. I don't have a lot of good memories of this place."

"You don't like me."

"No."

She smiled. "You and your brother look so much like your father."

His jaw ached from clenching it. "I don't really think you want to talk about that, do you?"

"Brand called. He'll be here tomorrow and will be staying on the ranch."

Cordell couldn't help being surprised. He'd called his father after he'd received the letter from his grandmother, figuring Brand had gotten one, as well. He had. He'd been adamant about not coming back except for his mother's funeral and, even then, he wasn't sure about that.

Cordell's father never talked about the ranch or his childhood here. He'd thrown himself into raising his boys after their mother had taken off when they were babies. Brand never said it, but he blamed Pepper. She couldn't stand any of the women her sons brought home and made their lives hell until they couldn't take it anymore and bailed.

After the twins left home, Brand threw himself into work. To Cordell it seemed his father had spent his life running away from the past.

"I know everyone blames me for their unhappiness. Do you think it is fair though, blaming me for what your grandfather did?" There was an edge to his grandmother's voice, a blade of both anger and pain.

"You were the *mother*. Mothers are supposed to protect their children."

He was instantly reminded of photographs of the children who'd been abducted from this area. "You didn't protect my father."

"No, I didn't. I let Call discipline them."

"Until Trace came along. What was it about him that made you protect him and not the others?"

She actually looked uncomfortable. "I was older. I felt as if I'd lost the others a long time ago. I guess you could say I drew a line in the sand."

Cordell laughed. "Is that what you call it? I'd always heard that my grandfather rode off one day and just never returned. Apparently that wasn't the case, huh. And, no, I don't believe for a moment that Alfred Hoagland killed my grandfather."

"His wife, Enid, swears that is the case."

He shook his head. "Why don't we cut to the chase? What do you want? You didn't invite me and Cyrus back here out of the goodness of your heart. Or because you're dying. You don't have a sentimental bone in your body."

She lifted her chin, body erect, and he saw a steely gleam in her dark eyes. She was still a beautiful woman, graceful and elegant, but cold and unfeeling, no matter what she said. "You might be surprised. Jack has already told me that you boys were in the third-floor room the day Trace was murdered," she said, her voice strong. "I need to know what you saw."

He wasn't sure what he'd expected her to ask him. Not this. That awful room was where his father and aunt and uncles had been sent as punishment. He and his brother had been forbidden to go to the room so of course they'd sneaked up there. *"Saw?"*

"Jack told me that you and your brother had a pair of small binoculars that you were arguing over."

Jack, the nanny's son? "Why would you believe anything Jack—"

"He's my grandson." She smiled wryly. "Those rumors about the nanny and my son Angus? They were true."

Cordell shook his head. "What a family."

"Yes, isn't it?" She lifted her cane and pointed toward the window. "See that ridge over there? That's where Trace was murdered."

His eyes widened. He'd had no idea his uncle had been killed within sight of the ranch. No wonder she was asking about this. From the third-floor room with a pair of binoculars was it possible one of them could have witnessed the murder? Apparently his grandmother thought so.

"I didn't see anything."

She nodded solemnly. "What about your brother?"

He shrugged. "You're going to have to ask him." He felt that awful pain and fought the thought that if Cyrus had seen something, they might never know. Cyrus might never regain consciousness. "What is it you think he might have seen? I thought Uncle Trace's killer was caught."

"Yes, but died after suggesting there was a co-conspirator."

That took him by surprise. "If Cyrus had seen a murder, he would have said something."

His grandmother didn't look convinced. "Not if he'd seen someone from this family on that ridge that day."

"If you think my father—"

"I didn't say it was Brand. Cyrus might have been so shocked that it was a family member he might not have dared tell. I know there were more children in that third-floor room than just you and Cyrus and Jack. Who else was up there?"

Cordell shook his head. "I just remember the three of us." He could feel his grandmother's gaze boring into him. She knew he was lying. He wasn't sure why after all these years he was still keeping the secret.

Because he'd promised. It was that simple.

The question was, how had his grandmother found out? Had Jack told that there had been two girls, one a year younger than him and her kid sister? They had ridden their horses over from the ranch down the road and he and Cyrus had sneaked them up into the room.

His grandmother would have gone ballistic had she known they were in the house. Pepper had never liked any of the neighboring ranchers—not that any of them were close by. But she'd especially disliked the McCormicks.

When she didn't come out and ask about the girls, he realized Jack hadn't told.

That made Cordell feel better about his "cousin" Jack.

"I called the hospital," his grandmother said. "There is no change in Cyrus's condition."

Cordell said nothing. He'd checked his cell phone on the way downstairs. There'd been no messages. That meant no news.

"Is that all?" he asked, getting to his feet.

His grandmother nodded, though she didn't look pleased.

Now at least he knew why she'd invited them all back to the ranch. She was looking for a traitor in the Winchester family.

Cordell smiled to himself at that as he headed back upstairs. Didn't she know that you couldn't throw a rock around here without hitting someone with traitorous motives?

RAINE TURNED ON THE tub water and poured in a shot of bubble bath, waiting until she was sure Cordell and the old housekeeper had gone downstairs before she pulled out her cell phone. No service. Tossing it back into her purse, she opened her small laptop. It only took a moment to get online via satellite.

Just as she suspected there would be, there was an e-mail from Marias.

"Get in touch."

She replied through instant messaging. "No cell service. What's up?"

A few moments later. "Winchesters squeaky clean, good rep, tough and damned good-looking from their photos on their Web site."

Raine shook her head, smiling as she got up to turn off the water in the tub. It was just like Marias to check them out to see just how handsome they were.

"So nothing to worry about, right?" she typed when she returned to her computer.

"Doesn't look that way."

They'd apparently taken time off from work to come visit their grandma. Except Cordell hadn't wanted to and couldn't wait to get out of here. She wondered how things were going downstairs with the two of them.

No reason to be suspicious of the Winchester brothers apparently.

"But you did get another package from Montana."

Raine jumped, startled by the tap on her door.

"Raine?"

Cordell.

She typed, "I assume you opened it."

Marias typed a smiley face.

"What's in it?"

"A crude map. Almost looks like a kid drew it. I think it might be a map to the house."

Raine felt her heart clutch in her chest. "Can you e-mail it to me?"

"Could take a few minutes."

Cordell tapped again, then she heard the creak of the hardwood floor as he went across the hall. She listened to the sound of a key in the lock, his door opening and closing, then silence.

In the bathroom, she tested the water. Still hot. The room was steamy. She closed the door and stripped off her clothing before gingerly stepping into the tub and sinking down in the scented bubbles.

She felt confused and unsure. Trust came hard for her. But in her job she'd become good at reading people. Did she still believe Cordell and his brother had been hired by someone to set her up?

She sank down deeper in the tub. She was starting to trust him and that scared her more than she wanted to admit. What if she was wrong?

That answer was simple. She would never leave Whitehorse, Montana.

In the other room, she heard the sound of another e-mail alert.

The map? With a chill she sank deeper in the water, terrified of what might be waiting for her at some remote house used by the child abductors.

SHERIFF MCCALL WINCHESTER wasn't surprised when Cordell called to say he'd found Raine Chandler and gotten his brother's pickup back. She was surprised, though, to see he was calling from a landline—at the Winchester Ranch.

"I still want to question her about your brother's assault," she told him, suspecting that her private investigator cousin had already done that.

"It sounds like it was an accident. Cyrus was just at the wrong place at the wrong time," he said.

"Uh-huh. Still... Do you know where I can reach her?" She heard him hesitate.

"We're waiting for the roads to dry out," he said finally.

"Oh?" McCall said. So there was more to this story, just as she'd suspected.

"After what happened last night, Raine was upset. I thought coming out here would get her mind off it."

Raine, huh? "Did Ms. Chandler say what she's doing in Whitehorse?"

"She's a journalist. Doing a story up this way."

"Know what about?"

"Didn't really get into that much."

McCall bit her tongue. "Could you ask her to stop by my office when you get back to town? Or better yet, let me ask her."

"She's in the bathtub across the hall in her room," he said, making McCall smile at how careful he was to make it clear she had her own room.

"Well, then why don't you have her stop by my office," McCall said. "I heard your father is coming to the ranch tomorrow. Grandmother invited me out for dinner. I hope you'll be there. I assume Aunt Virginia is still there?"

"Haven't seen her."

"Dinner should be interesting."

"More like pure hell. I wouldn't count on me being there. Is there anything new on the dark-colored van and the man driving it?"

"We found the van. It had been stolen from Havre. Forensics will be coming in tomorrow to see what they can find. I'll let you know if they come up with anything." McCall hung up, irritated with her cousin but sympathetic.

Earlier she'd stopped by the hospital. Cyrus was still in a coma. She picked up the report the deputy had given her on the altercation in the parking lot behind the hotel, anxious to talk to Raine Chandler.

Something was definitely wrong. McCall hoped her cousin knew what he was doing taking Raine to the ranch. She feared he didn't have a clue who the woman was—or what she was capable of, for that matter.

After all, he believed she was a journalist up here on a story.

IMPATIENT AFTER HIS CALL to the sheriff, Cordell turned on the television but he couldn't find a channel that could hold his attention so he just left it on the news and turned down the volume.

He began to go through the information again that Raine had collected on missing children. It was shocking and he suspected it was only the tip of the iceberg.

He found an article from a psychologist who dealt with the children who were recovered from child molesters. "Trust is devastated. Often the victim is made to feel responsible for what happened. They feel powerless, trapped. That sense of learned helplessness can last a lifetime." He skimmed the rest, words jumping out at him. *Humiliation. Alienation. Trauma. Vulnerability. Psychological shock. Postvictimization.*

He got to his feet. He couldn't read anymore. He had so many questions he wanted to ask Raine. What was taking her so long? She hadn't seemed like the kind of woman who would lounge around in the bath this long.

Picking up the Emily Frank file, he saw that she'd been a foster child. He realized he knew nothing about foster care. Sitting down, he began to read.

A line jumped out at him. "Children in foster care live in an uncertain world. They lack the stability and permanence that other children take for granted and are often moved at a moment's notice, all of their belongings fitting into no more than a plastic grocery bag."

He could relate to that. He and his twin had moved constantly from the time they were seven until they were able to go away to college. His father, Brand Winchester, was a quiet, taciturn man who worked as a ranch manager, moving like the wind from one job to the next. He'd never remarried after the twins' mother had left them when the boys were babies.

Brand never blamed his mother for the failure of his marriage or his life, but it was unspoken.

Cordell and Cyrus had been old enough to remember the day their grandmother had kicked them all off the ranch where they'd lived since they were born. He and Cyrus had learned at an early age to give their grandmother a wide berth, spending their days outside as much as possible with the horses or playing in the barn or outbuildings.

The family had scattered like fall leaves after that, none of his father's siblings keeping in touch except once in a long while. At least he and Cyrus had each other and had never been abandoned by their father.

Looking back though, Cordell realized how they could have ended up in foster care if things hadn't worked out for his father once they'd left the ranch and the only life his father had known.

His gaze settled again on the words in front of him.

"Foster children's lives are about leaving behind things and friends and places they know, their lives haunted by neglect and child abuse. In foster care they often lose their sense of identity."

He picked up a grainy newspaper photograph of Emily Frank. The girl was wearing a dress that was too big for her. She looked gangly and a little too thin, but she wore a beatific smile.

He saw something he hadn't noticed before. A tiny silver horse pin. Even in the photograph he could see that it was in an odd place because of a small tear in the fabric that not even the pin could hide.

His heart ached for the little girl. According to the foster home paperwork, Emily had been kicked around from one foster home to another since she was two and had only been at the new foster home in Whitehorse one night. Before that she'd run away from her last foster home.

He could see how the foster parents might have thought she'd run away this time, too. They wouldn't have acted right away, a huge mistake.

He wondered how she'd ended up in foster care to begin with. Maybe Raine would know. He glanced toward his door, wondering how long before she finished her bath. He was anxious to find these monsters and hoped to hell Raine had a plan other than using herself as bait.

The tap at his door startled him. He quickly put everything back in the satchel and went to answer the door.

Raine stood out in the hall, her hair damp, her face

glowing from her bath. She hadn't taken the time to put on that awful white makeup or the dark eyeliner. He marveled at how young and clean and fresh she looked without it. Like a different woman.

It struck him that she used the makeup almost like a mask—or a disguise. Was it possible Raine had known this girl Emily Frank? He felt his pulse quicken. Was it possible she'd been a foster child at the Amberson house when Emily was taken?

That, he realized in a flash, would explain why she wrote about these abducted children, why she knew so much about foster children, why she'd come all this way to do a story on Emily Frank.

"Is everything all right with your grandmother?" she asked, and he realized he must have been frowning as he wondered about her. "Is she upset about me staying here?"

"No, she is more interested in the past than the present. I don't want to talk about her, if you don't mind." He sighed and motioned for her to come in, reminding himself that it didn't matter if Raine had a connection to Emily Frank or not.

All that mattered was finding the bastard who'd put his brother in a coma.

The moment the door closed behind her, he demanded, "How do we find these people?"

RAINE HAD SEEN THE WAY he was looking at her and regretted that she hadn't taken the time to put on her makeup.

But she wrote off his behavior as impatience the moment he spoke. He just wanted to find the man who'd hurt his brother. On that they could agree.

"Emily had just come to Whitehorse the night before so only a limited number of people knew about her," she said. "From her diary, I think it is clear that her abductors knew she was a new foster child. They might even have been tipped off by the foster parents or possibly the social worker."

"You can't really believe they were in on this?"

Did she? "Everyone is a suspect and they knew Emily had run away from her last two foster homes. Emily Frank had unknowingly made herself the perfect abduction victim."

"Last *two* foster homes? I only read about one that she ran away from."

Raine sighed. He'd been studying the material while she was gone and was just looking for discrepancies. "The other foster family kept it quiet. It reflects poorly on the foster family if the children run away, but you'll find it in the social worker's report." She stepped to the table and pulled it out of the stack of papers to hand it to him.

He looked chastised. "How did she end up in foster care anyway?"

"The way a lot of them do. Single mom. Dad never in the picture. Mom deemed unfit. The state takes the girl in the middle of the night and puts her in foster care with complete strangers."

"Why was the mother deemed unfit?"

"All it said on the report I was able to get was child endangerment. Could have been anything." She glanced from him to the television and froze.

"I have to admit I knew nothing about foster children until I started reading the material you'd gathered…" His voice trailed off as he finally noticed that she was no longer listening. "Raine?"

She groped blindly for the remote, unable to take her eyes off the newscaster and the words streaming across the bottom of the television screen.

CORDELL SAW HER REACHING for the television remote and turned to look at the television screen. A woman newscaster was standing in the Whitehorse Hotel parking lot. He thought it must be a story about last night's hit-and-run—until he caught the words running along the bottom of the screen and felt as if he'd been punched in the stomach.

Raine turned up the volume an instant later, the news commentator's voice filling the room.

"The girl disappeared from her home last night."

Out of the corner of his eye, Cordell saw Raine drop onto the edge of the bed with a sound like a wounded animal.

"Lara English had been playing hide-and-seek with her foster siblings at the time of her disappearance behind the Whitehorse Hotel. One of the children reported seeing a dark-colored van leaving the area shortly before hearing sirens."

"What the hell?" Cordell said under his breath. It couldn't be a coincidence that a child had been abducted from behind the hotel—the same area where Raine had nearly been run down and his brother struck by someone driving a dark-colored van.

"The foster mother, believing the child was hiding or had run away, didn't call the sheriff's department until late today."

An angry-looking woman came on the screen. "You don't know this kid. I do. So of course I thought she was just hiding from the other kids and refusing to come out or that she'd run. What was I supposed to think? You have no idea what some of these foster kids are like. No idea."

Lara English's photo flashed on the television screen.

"Hell," Cordell said on a shocked breath. He stared at the photograph that came up on the screen. The girl was blonde, blue-eyed and grinning into the camera. He felt his heart drop like a stone. The girl looked enough like Emily Frank to be her sister.

The news report ended with the usual. "If anyone sees this nine-year-old girl, please call the sheriff's department." The number flashed on the screen.

His cousin McCall came on in uniform and encouraged anyone with information to contact her immediately.

As the news changed to the construction of a new bridge in Great Falls, he took the remote from Raine's trembling fingers and turned off the television.

"Okay, no more lies. What the hell is going on?" he demanded even though he could see she was in as much shock as he was. "And don't tell me it doesn't have something to do with you."

RAINE STARED AT THE blank television, her heart racing as if she'd just had to run for her life. She tried to breathe but couldn't seem to catch her breath.

She could still see the little girl's face that had only moments before been on the television screen. Emily Frank. No, she thought with a mental shake, only a child who looked enough like Emily to—

"Raine? *Raine!*"

She blinked and dragged her gaze away from the now blank television screen.

Cordell handed her a paper cup half full of cold water. "Here, drink some of this." She took a sip, hating how weak and afraid she felt, how helpless. He motioned for her to finish it.

She did and he took the empty cup from her trembling hand. Her mind seemed scattered as she watched him ball up the cup and throw it into the trash. He came back to kneel in front of her.

"These are the same people who took Emily Frank, aren't they?" he said, taking both of her hands in his.

She was aware of the warmth of his hands and how her cold ones seemed to disappear in his. She looked up into his dark eyes and wondered how she'd ever thought them cold and unfeeling. There was heartbreak in them.

Raine wanted to pull back from the pain she saw there. It too closely mirrored her own.

"Talk to me," he said quietly. Of course he'd seen the resemblance between Lara English and Emily Frank. He knew it had been no coincidence they looked so much alike.

Raine felt sick to her stomach. Cordell knew, just as she did, that this was about *her.* It had been from the moment she'd received the lined pages torn from Emily's school notebook. "They took that girl because of me."

"Why would they do that?" Cordell asked. "It can't be because of some magazine article. You were a foster child, weren't you?"

With her gaze locked to his, she knew she didn't have to answer. He'd seen the answer.

"You knew Emily Frank?"

Raine shivered and dragged her gaze away to look toward the French door she'd left partially cracked open earlier. A cool breeze blew in. She watched it stir the row of tall old cottonwoods flanking the massive log lodge. Beyond them was a huge red barn and horses in a summer-green pasture.

Not even that picturesque scene, though, could lift the horrible weight resting on her chest. How was it she could feel for these lost children, but she couldn't appreciate beauty or feel love? Because something had died in her sixteen years ago the day Emily Frank was taken.

She turned back to Cordell, surprised at the tears that

brimmed in her eyes and the sobbing ache that hitched in her chest. "I am Emily Frank. That's why they took that girl. Because of me."

Chapter Seven

Cordell stared at her in disbelief. "That can't be. Emily Frank is dead."

"That's what a lot of people believed especially after Orville Cline confessed to her abduction and murder," she said, slipping her hands from his as she rose to go to the window.

Cordell shuddered as he recalled the graphic description in Orville's confession as to how he killed her and what he did with her body.

"Emily escaped," she said, her back to him. "They never found her. Then a week ago I got the pages from Emily's notebook."

He rose to his feet, unsure what to do or say. He couldn't help noticing the way she was talking about Emily as if she was a separate person from her. He suspected that was the way she thought of her. But now, at least, he knew the connection.

Outside, a fierce warm wind howled across the eaves. In this part of the country, the weather changed in an instant, often with huge ranges in temperature, as well.

The roads would be drying out. For once, luck was

with them, he thought, since this latest news had changed everything.

"Emily was one of those foster kids bounced from home to home from the age of two," Raine said. "She never knew her father. She could barely remember her mother, a teenager who dumped her at strange people's houses so she could go out partying with her friends. From such a young age, it makes a kid resilient."

"Still—"

"It's amazing the way we're able to accept what happens to us," she said. "We don't know any differently. It isn't as if we have that much contact with kids from normal families."

Cordell couldn't believe that. She would have seen other children at school or in the neighborhood who had a father and mother, families, secure lives that didn't change in an instant.

He frowned as it all began to sink in. "You're not a journalist on a story."

She shook her head, her gaze settling on his. "I'm a private investigator in L.A."

"A *private investigator?*" Small world. But that explained a lot, including the gun she carried and how she'd managed to get away from him at the hotel this morning.

"If you don't believe me you can call my partner, Marias Alvarez."

"I believe you." He realized he did. Just as he'd believed her confession about being Emily Frank. "How did Emily get away?"

She stood silhouetted against the afternoon light, her back to him. Earlier she'd looked defeated, but now there was a new strength to her, a new determination as she turned suddenly to face him.

He wondered how many times this woman had been forced to find that strength. Cordell couldn't bear the thought of what she'd been through.

"When Emily was found more than two hundred miles from Whitehorse, she was near death. No one knows how she got there. She didn't speak for two months and when she did, she had no memory of what had happened to her."

"My God," Cordell said and hoped with all his heart that she would never have any memory of what had happened to her. "We have to go to the sheriff."

"If we do, he'll kill Lara right away. You have to trust me on this. If you go to the sheriff, it will cost Lara her life and I fear it will be the last I hear from the person sending me the information."

Cordell didn't doubt she knew what she was talking about. But what if she was wrong? "What are you saying? The person who sent you those pages just got you back here to kill you."

She shook her head. "Why would they do that? Orville Cline had already confessed to Emily's murder."

"Maybe they're worried that your memory has come back and are afraid you can identify them."

RAINE HESITATED, then said, "I still believe that one of them wants this to stop and is helping me to bring the child abductor down." She told him that her friend and partner Marias Alvarez called the person CBA or Crazy Bastard Abductor. "I think Crazy Bitch Abductor might be closer to the truth. I believe it's the wife sending me the information and that she got me back here because she knows she can't stop him without help."

"That's some theory. I hope it doesn't get you killed."

"What choice do I have? There's a little girl out there missing. I have to find her before it is too late," she said, her voice breaking. The news about the latest little girl had chilled her to her very bones. She knew exactly what Lara English was going through.

But she couldn't give in to her emotions. She had to be strong. "I have to put all my energy into finding Lara."

"And you believe this CBA will help you do that," he said, sounding more than a little skeptical.

"Now that he's taken Lara, I have to believe it," she said.

Cordell studied her for a long moment and she could see he was considering her argument. "You do realize that he knows someone leaked you the information. That's how he knew where you'd be last night when he took Lara."

She nodded solemnly. "That means the woman could be in as much trouble as Lara. Another reason we have to find them and Lara before it's too late."

"How do you suggest we do that?"

"The Crazy Bitch Abductor sent us a map."

"I HOPE THIS MAP MAKES more sense to you than it does to me," Cordell said as Raine stared at her computer on the way to Whitehorse.

The wind dried the top of the road bed. As long as he avoided the mud puddles, the rental car got enough traction to keep them out of the ditch.

Before they'd left the ranch, he'd called to have a wrecker pull out his brother's pickup. He planned to pick it up in town. For these Montana roads, a truck worked much better. He'd also called the hospital. There was no change in Cyrus's condition.

"I would assume it's a map to the house where my abductors took me sixteen years ago," Raine said.

The map was crude at best, hand-drawn as if by a child. He felt a chill the first time she'd showed it to him back at the ranch. He'd had to agree with her when he'd seen it. Maybe someone was trying to help her. Or not.

"I still think we should go the sheriff," he'd argued when he'd seen the map. "McCall needs to know what's going on."

"Your cousin is already searching for Lara. She's a cop. Don't you think she's already considered that Lara might have been abducted? Especially after what went down behind the Whitehorse Hotel last night?"

He'd agreed that she was right and he didn't want to take a chance with Raine's life any more than he did Lara's. The problem was he didn't trust whoever was sending her this information.

Raine was the only one they knew of who'd gotten

away from her abductors in this area. Orville Cline had confessed to her murder. Raine was living proof of his lie—and knew that he hadn't taken her.

Wasn't that more than enough motive to get her back to where it had all happened to tie up the loose end in the cruelest of all ways? By making her relive her abduction through Lara English?

His heart broke for the child Raine had been just as it did for Lara. He swore he would see that these people paid—or he'd die trying.

"You don't think this house is where he took Lara, do you?" Cordell asked.

"No. The CBA would be too afraid to give that up—if she even knows. No, I think there is something at the house on the map that she wants me to find, though."

He glanced over at her, hearing the fear in her voice she was trying hard to hide. "You never told me what happened after you were found miles from Whitehorse," he said, not comfortable with his own thoughts right now.

But he needed to know everything about Emily Frank if he planned to help Raine. When she didn't answer, he glanced over at her. "I'm sorry, if you'd rather not tell me—"

"No. I want to tell you. If I had come forward before this, maybe Lara English wouldn't have been abducted."

"You can't remember what your abductors look like," he pointed out. "And as you said, these people are chameleons, blending in with society. All you would have done was put yourself in the line of fire earlier."

RAINE COULDN'T ARGUE THAT, but the truth was she hadn't been ready to face this. She wasn't sure she was now.

But she knew she had to be honest with Cordell if they hoped to find Lara before it was too late. Together they might stand a chance, a slim one, but at least a chance. And she knew he had a lot of questions. Anyone would.

"I told you Emily didn't remember anything. That wasn't true."

"Raine, you don't have to—"

"I don't remember what they looked like. Either I didn't see their faces or I didn't want to remember them. That night while the thunder and lightning boomed around me, I wrote the pages in my notebook to keep myself calm. I guess that's when the idea came to me how I could escape."

"You didn't try before that?"

She shook her head and smiled over at him.

"I can't imagine having the presence of mind to do that. Not at age ten. I would have cried and screamed myself hoarse."

"You never know what you would do in a situation like that," she said. "I was a foster child. I'd been thrown into so many uncomfortable situations, I don't think I was as terrified as a child who'd never known adversity.

Also I was used to being alone and pretty much taking care of myself."

"What happened after you escaped?"

"I found my way to the highway, followed it until I came to a farmhouse. It was early in the morning. I hid in the back of a pickup that was running in the yard. After the truck pulled out of the yard, I fell asleep curled under an old tarp and when I woke up I was in a town I had never seen before.

"As it turned out, I was in Williston, North Dakota, not even in Montana any longer, hundreds of miles away from Whitehorse. When the driver went inside a store, I climbed out of the back of the truck. I must have been a real mess when a nice woman found me. I was running a fever, sick and weak. They were afraid I wouldn't survive."

"They didn't know you and how strong you are," he said, his voice filled with admiration.

Raine felt her face heat from it and hurried on with her story. "The Chandlers took me in. It was Mrs. Chandler who'd found me and got me medical attention. They say I didn't speak for months and by then I was smart enough to make up a story so I never had to go back to that foster home in Whitehorse. I think I knew I would be abducted again or sent away to possibly somewhere worse."

"The Chandlers were nice to you?"

"Tom and Minnie Chandler were in their forties. Their only son was away at college. I think they were thankful to have a child under their roof. They adopted me after a time. They let me chose my own name. Raine seemed appropriate since the storm was what had saved me."

Cordell shook his head, awed by her story. "They never put it together that you were Emily Frank, this girl missing from a town just across the hi-line a few hundred miles?"

"Emily was believed to have run away. There wasn't much of a network for missing children sixteen years ago. That was before Amber Alert. And as I've said, from my experience, foster children often run away or fall through the cracks. I'd only been with the Ambersons in Whitehorse one night. They didn't know anything about me except that I'd run away from the last two homes I'd been in."

"You're saying they weren't invested in looking for you." He couldn't believe what he was hearing. "So there wasn't much of a search for you. Still you would think that someone in Williston would have heard about the missing girl. The Chandlers had to wonder why no one was looking for you."

She smiled. "When Minnie found me, I was wearing a hand-me-down worn dress that was too big for me and no shoes. I think she realized when no one came looking for me that I was better off with her and that's why she didn't try to find out where I came from."

Cordell's thought exactly. "I'm glad they were good to you. They must have been relieved when Orville Cline confessed to abducting and killing Emily Frank. They probably thought you were safe."

"We all did," Raine said. "I was at college when I read about Orville Cline's arrest and his confessions. I wanted to believe he was the one. It was easier than believing that the people were still out there, still taking little girls. I thought he lied about killing…" her voice caught "…Emily because he didn't want anyone looking for me. It never dawned on me that he could have made a deal with my abductors."

Cordell heard the pain in her voice, the guilt. "You can't blame yourself. After what you'd been through, you had to know that if you did anything, they could find you."

"But they still found me, didn't they?"

"How? That's what I don't understand," he said.

"I've been asking myself that. I assume someone put two and two together in Williston."

"Is it possible the truck driver saw you when you got out of the back of his pickup?"

"Maybe. I jumped out and ran and hid. But wouldn't you think he would have told someone?"

"Maybe he did. Maybe he told your foster parents back in Whitehorse, but since it appeared you'd merely run away…"

Raine nodded. "I've known all along I would have to talk to them eventually. But first I have to see where this map leads me."

Cordell could hear how anxious she was as he looked down the road they'd just turned down and wondered where they were being led—and, more to the point, by whom?

He saw Raine glance at her watch. She'd told him that if Lara could be found within seventy-two hours, she stood the best chance of being found alive.

They'd already lost precious hours. He could almost hear the clock ticking.

Chapter Eight

Cordell looked out at the growing darkness, his anxiety growing.

"According to the map, it's just a little farther," Raine said in the pickup cab next to him. "He wouldn't want the house to be too far from town and yet far enough away and remote enough that he knew no one would accidentally stumble across it."

Cordell had insisted they stop in Whitehorse long enough to trade the rental car for the pickup. The moment he'd realized the roads would be passable that they could leave the ranch, he'd called a towing service in town.

The wrecker had gotten to the pickup in the ditch, just minutes before they did. They'd followed the tow truck driver into town and made the switch, losing only a little daylight.

From Highway 2 they'd turned off a dirt road, then another, each road getting smaller and less used until now they were in a creek bottom of narrow ravines, rocky bluffs and twisting juniper-choked coulees.

"The next turn should be up here on the right," Raine said.

"I don't see a road," he said, squinting through the twilight. Deep shadows hunkered in the underbrush along the creek.

"There it is." Just then a whitetail deer bolted from the brush and ran directly in front of the pickup, startling them both. He hit the brakes. Raine let out a breath as the deer swept past unhurt.

Cordell didn't like the closed-in feel of this river bottom. Nor did he trust that whoever had sent Raine the map was interested in confessing and ending this. Ending this, maybe. But with someone dying and he feared that someone the informant had in mind was Raine Chandler, aka Emily Frank.

The road dropped down into a thicket of stunted aspen trees along the creek bottom. A perfect place for an ambush, he thought as he pulled a pistol from under his brother's seat, checked the clip and rested the weapon next to him as he turned down the road.

He noticed that Raine had apparently thought the same thing as she already had her gun resting in her hand, no doubt loaded and ready to fire. It made him feel a little better to realize that she wasn't putting all of her trust in this CBA.

She'd tucked away the computer and lowered her window. The air smelled of summer, the grasses tall and green. A wisp of cloud floated along on the breeze against the pale twilight.

It was one of those perfect Montana summer evenings.

He wanted to breathe it all in, to stop by the creek and watch stars come out in the awe-inspiring big sky. He wanted more than anything to not go around the next bend.

Instead, they were on the hunt for monsters, the worst kind, the kind who hurt children. Just knowing the man and woman who'd hurt Raine were so close by made him homicidal. He feared if he didn't get them first, they would get Raine.

As he drove around the bend in the road, he saw the house. Raine saw it, too. She let out a heartbreaking sound. This, he knew, was where her abductors had brought her sixteen years ago.

RAINE THOUGHT SHE WAS prepared. For so long the abduction had been buried deep enough that she really hadn't been able to remember anything. Parts of it had come back over the years.

But there were still holes in her memory, holes she wasn't so sure she shouldn't leave empty and dark.

Unfortunately, her instincts told her that the only way she'd be able to find Lara was if she remembered everything.

As the pickup's headlights swept over the abandoned old farmhouse, the past washed over her, taking her breath away, sending her heart hammering as she smelled the dank darkness, felt the aching cold, heard the sound of the door opening. And closing. She knew this house.

"Stop!"

Cordell hit the brakes as she threw open her door.

She heard him call to her to wait, but the house pulled her to it, metal to magnet. It was as if she no longer could hold back the nightmare. Sixteen years ago she'd believed she would die in this house.

Behind her, she heard Cordell running after her.

As she neared the house, she thought she tasted blood.

The cut lip. She'd forgotten about that, but not about the woman who'd smacked her and told her she'd better do everything the man told her if she knew what was good for her.

The door to the old place was partially open, a sliver of darkness gaping behind it.

Cordell caught up with her, shoved a flashlight into her hand. She looked over at him, grateful. He wasn't going to try to stop her. He knew nothing could, not even him.

He played the light over the front step with his flashlight, then into the dank musty interior. She turned hers on and moved up the creaking steps. Her fingers ached as she touched the door. It swung open with a creak that sent a blade of ice into her heart. A blast of cold, putrid air rushed out at her.

"Let me go in first," he whispered as he stepped past her.

The door yawned all the way open. The smell triggered thoughts and feelings and fears that made her pulse pound in her ears and legs weak beneath her. She clutched her gun in one hand, the flashlight in the other and told herself she could do this. She was the little girl who'd survived. She was Emily Frank.

She'd put off facing this all these years. Now she had no choice. The clue to where they'd find Lara English was here. Why else lead her here?

To kill you?

No, she thought as she followed Cordell inside the house. Taunt her, maybe. Terrify her, absolutely. But ultimately, the answer was here.

The house seemed full of whispers and skittering sounds, creaks and groans. One dark room after another appeared in the beam of their flashlights until she reached the stairs that dropped down into the partial basement.

"Hell, no," Cordell said beside her.

PEPPER WINCHESTER STOOD in the third-floor room in the dark. She didn't want to turn on the lights. This evening she wasn't up to reading what her children had scratched in the walls.

She'd been coming up here for weeks now. As some form of punishment for her sins? Or just because she had nowhere else to go?

In this room was where she'd let her husband, Call, send their children. It was small and always made her feel closed in. There was a window that faced out toward the ridge where her youngest son had been murdered.

She looked out it now, barely able to make out the ridge in the growing darkness. It came to her why, after so many years, she'd begun to frequent this horrible reminder of her failure as a mother. It was also a reminder that one of her children had betrayed her in the worst possible way.

One of her children had helped with the murder of his—or her—youngest sibling. And to make matters worse, she feared one of her own grandchildren had witnessed it from this very room—and kept quiet all these years.

A rustling sound startled her. Her hand went to her throat before she realized it was only the party hats that had ended up huddled in the far corner. There must be a breeze coming up from the elevator shaft.

It was the party hats that had clued her into the fact that her grandchildren had been in this room the day of Trace's murder. Trace, her youngest, her most precious, her favorite. He had died on that far ridge the day of his birthday.

Pepper blamed herself, this house, this life, her long-dead husband, Call. Trace's alleged killer was dead. But in her heart she believed that her son's true killer remained free and unknown. At least for the time being.

At the sound of a car engine, she turned to see lights coming up the narrow ranch road. Brand. She hadn't seen her son for twenty-seven years, had yet to speak to him since the day she'd sent him away and all the others when Trace hadn't shown for his birthday party.

She knew her children had reason to hate her. She'd taken away their birthright: Winchester Ranch.

But that was the least of what she'd deprived them of over their lives.

In the last of the day's light, she fumbled for the elevator button. The door opened, she shoved aside the gate and stepped into an even smaller space. Heart pounding and her breath coming in gasps, she descended to the ground floor and hurriedly got out, her cane tapping on the wood floor.

She knew the kind of reception she would get from her son Brand. Like his son Cordell, he hated her, blamed her, wanted nothing to do with her.

Pepper had only one hope as she hurried to greet him. Out of her five children, she hoped Brand wasn't the one who'd betrayed his brother.

"I HAVE TO GO DOWN THERE," Raine said as she took a step down the stairs.

Cordell heard both pleading and determination in her tone. The message was clear: *Please don't try to stop me.* He doubted he could even if he tried.

He shone his flashlight into the cold damp darkness below the house and cringed. He wouldn't have kept a dog down there, let alone a child.

He'd done his best not to imagine where Lara English was being held. But seeing this partial basement, which in truth was nothing more than a crawl space, he could imagine the horrible place that little girl was in right now. Alone? Or were they with her?

He shuddered at the thought and followed on Raine's heels into the pit below.

She stopped suddenly, the beam of her flashlight flickering over a pile of old lumber. Raine played the light over the boards, then the wooden slats of the wall behind it. Cordell kept his flashlight pointed at his feet, trying to stay out of her way. He didn't doubt that this was something she needed to do. He couldn't imagine what thoughts and emotions were going through her head right now.

Suddenly she seemed to sway on her feet. He reached for her and saw in the ambient glow of their flashlights that her eyes were as vacant as this old house.

"Raine?" He couldn't help the fear that gripped him. *"Raine?"*

She didn't answer, but blinked and her face contorted in a mask of pain. Dear God, she was reliving what had happened to her down here.

"Raine!" He grabbed her arm and shook her. Her eyes fluttered and he watched as she fought her way to the surface, gasping for breath, a high keening sound coming from her lips.

He could see the memories trying to pull her back under, a riptide wanting to take her, drown her.

He dragged her into his arms, holding her, saying her name over and over. "Raine. Raine." But he feared she was Emily Frank again and there was no bringing her back.

A few moments later she surfaced and seemed surprised to find herself in his arms. "What happened?"

Cordell shook his head. He didn't have a clue.

She closed her eyes and for a moment, he thought he'd lost her again.

"I remember," she said in a hoarse whisper. "I wasn't

molested. Only because I fought back. Only because I would have preferred to die than let that man touch me again." Her eyes opened and he'd never been so relieved to see that sea of clear blue. "I bit him. Cordell, are you listening to me? I bit the man who abducted me. I bit his left hand so hard there is no way I didn't leave a scar."

He was too busy thinking how relieved he was that she was her old self again.

The realization of what she was saying finally sank in. A scar. It might be a way to identify the man. If they ever got that close to him.

Raine stepped toward the wall behind the small pile of old lumber. Her flashlight beam scoured the boards, then froze on a spot.

He stepped closer.

It had been sixteen years so the letters scratched in the wall were almost too faint to read. When he did make them out, he wished he hadn't. His insides seemed to liquefy and he knew he would remember those words until the day he died.

There carved in the wood was, *Emily Frank died here.*

Chapter Nine

Emily Frank's former foster family was just finishing dinner. The night breeze carried the scent of boiled chicken and root vegetables.

Cordell noticed that Raine seemed to hang back as they neared the large rambling farmhouse even though he doubted the couple would recognize her—not after sixteen years. Also she'd changed her appearance from the blonde little girl they would remember, having dyed her hair dark.

The only thing about her that was recognizable from the girl she'd been was her eyes. They were that incredible sky-blue, so clear they seemed infinite. He'd gotten lost in them enough to know just how unforgettable they were.

He could tell she was nervous about seeing her former foster parents again even though she'd spent only one night there. He knew she feared they might have been in on the abduction.

"The abduction was planned. It wasn't spur-of-the-moment," she'd told him on the way to town. "The couple who took me knew who I was. That means they'd known the Ambersons were getting a foster child."

"And not just any foster child," Cordell had said. "One who'd run away from the past two homes she'd been placed in."

Raine had looked over at him as if impressed that he was beginning to understand how this had gone down. Either that or she was wondering why it had taken him so long to figure things out.

"You all right?" he asked now. They'd parked down the road from the house, deciding to walk up the narrow lane that ended at the front door. Cordell had thought it would be easier on Raine.

The question seemed to jerk her out of her thoughts, her gaze going to the house's second story where a pink curtain billowed out the open window on the breeze.

"I was just wondering what makes people become foster parents," she said.

A love for children would have been his first guess— at least before he'd met Raine. A more cynical answer would be the money, though he couldn't imagine that foster parents were paid enough per child to make it worthwhile taking on children who often had problems—and were a problem.

"I would imagine there are some who are wonderful and feel they are called to do this," he said.

She nodded and gave him a wry smile. "I'd just like to know who called the Ambersons," she said under her breath.

As they neared, the screen door swung open and

a man stepped out onto the large porch. He smiled in greeting, squinting a little as he studied first Cordell and then Raine as if he thought he should know them. That was the thing about Whitehorse. Most everyone did know each other.

His eyes seemed to narrow before his gaze returned to Cordell.

"Good evening. Can I help you?" he asked. He had a deep, rich voice. His hands were large and callused and he looked strong and solid. A man who did physical labor, Cordell guessed.

"Abel Amberson?" The serious man was in his late fifties, graying at the temples, lines around his eyes and mouth more from being out in the sun than from laughing, Cordell thought.

Abel gave a slight nod, looking instantly wary.

"I'm Cordell Winchester. This is Raine Chandler. We're here about one of your former foster children."

The man arched a brow. "You aren't with Social Services."

"No. We're looking into the disappearance of Emily Frank," Cordell said.

"Emily?" he repeated, clearly taken aback.

"We hoped we could ask you some questions. I'm sure the local sheriff will be speaking with you as well about the latest abduction."

"Latest abduction?" asked a woman coming through the screen door. Grace Amberson was a small woman with a kind face and eyes. "Why would you be questioning *us?* She's not our foster child."

"No, but Emily Frank was," Raine said.

The woman's gaze swung to Raine and held there long enough Cordell thought she might have recognized her. "Emily wasn't abducted," Grace said. "She ran away."

"A child molester now serving time in prison confessed to taking Emily Frank," Cordell said.

Grace Amberson clasped both hands as she cried, "Emily wasn't taken by a child molester. What are these people talking about, Abel?" Her voice broke and tears welled in her eyes.

"The man's name is Orville Cline," Raine said. "Maybe you've heard of him."

Cordell knew she was watching for a reaction. She must have been disappointed.

"Who?" Abel asked. His wife showed no sign of recognition, either.

"Orville *Cline*. He confessed to abducting and killing Emily Frank."

"No, that's not possible," Grace cried, her voice filled with horror.

"Why don't you let me take care of this, Grace," her husband said quietly. Behind them a half-dozen children from about five to thirteen peered out from the screen. "Take the children in and give them some ice cream. I'll be in shortly."

"I'm sorry if we upset you," Raine said to Grace and smiled through the screen at the children. "Would you mind if I used your bathroom?"

Cordell could see that the woman wanted to say no but it wasn't in her nature.

"Of course." Grace held the door open behind her as Raine entered.

"I think you'd better show me some identification," Abel said the moment the women were gone. "You've upset my wife."

Cordell took his driver's license and P.I. license from his wallet and handed it to the man. "We're investigating the Emily Frank case for a client. Ms. Chandler and I are both private investigators."

Abel Amberson's eyes widened in surprise as he handed back the licenses. "This comes as a terrible shock. We were told she ran away."

"Who told you that?"

"Social Services and the sheriff at the time. She'd run away from two other foster homes. Was she really taken by this man?"

"According to him. His confession is very…detailed," Cordell said, putting his ID away and pocketing his wallet.

"Is that what they think happened to this other girl, Lara English?" Abel looked stricken. He glanced back toward his house as if worried about his family inside it. "Why hasn't someone warned us?"

Cordell shook his head. Probably because the local news media hadn't picked up on it. Emily Frank's abduction was one of a dozen crimes Orville had admitted to committing. Cordell wondered how many more the man had lied about.

The screen opened and Raine came out. She looked pale. "Ready?"

He nodded. "Well, thank you, Mr. Amberson, for your time." He held out his hand and Abel shook it. "If you think of anything that might help." Cordell handed him his business card. "My cell phone number is on the back."

As he and Raine walked down the narrow road to where they'd parked the pickup, Cordell could feel the tension coming off her like a live wire.

"Abel Amberson didn't have a scar on his left hand," he said once they were out of earshot.

"No, but I found something in the house," she said. "I was admiring the children's drawings tacked on the refrigerator when I saw an invitation to the Whitehorse Summer Gala. Apparently it is invitation only. That means only the cream of Whitehorse crop will be there tomorrow night."

Raine looked over at him as they reached the truck. "And care to guess who the guests of honor are this year? Abel and Ruth Amberson for their years of foster care. Do you think your grandmother can get us an invitation?"

FROM THE WINDOW, Pepper saw not just one son, but two climb from the car in front of the lodge. Both men were tall and handsome like their father.

Brand glanced toward the window where she stood and she braced herself. From his expression this was the last place on earth he wanted to be.

She shifted her gaze to her older son Worth, or Worthless, as Call had called him. It surprised her how old he looked. Both of her sons were in their fifties.

That was hard for her to accept, that, like her, they had aged. She remembered them as being strong and determined, wild as this land. She could see them riding across the ranch, young and free.

Guilt wedged itself into her heart as sharp and painful as a knife blade. What had she done to them? Turned them out, took away what they thought was their legacy: the Winchester Ranch.

Pepper straightened, setting her expression as she headed for the front door leaning more heavily than usual on her cane. Facing her sons would be harder than anything she'd ever done, she realized.

If only she was the cold, uncaring bitch they thought she was. It would make this so much easier.

As she reached the top of the stairs, she saw Virginia go to the door. She could tell by the set of her daughter's shoulders that she thought Brand and Worth were only here for the money, money she felt was owed to her.

Her old maid daughter, her oldest child and only girl, wore her bitterness like a shroud. That, too, Pepper thought, was her fault. Was it fear that made Virginia so greedy? Or did she really not care for anyone but herself?

Maybe she thought that with the Winchester fortune she wouldn't feel so alone. Of course, she was wrong. Her mother could attest to that.

At the door, Virginia gave her brothers awkward

hugs, then the three of them turned and looked up the stairs as if they'd sensed their mother watching them.

Pepper put steel in her back as she slowly descended the stairs. She could feel their gazes riveted on her, each of them wondering just how frail and close to death she was.

She kept her chin up. She wouldn't let them see the mountain of regret that lay on her chest, making it nearly impossible to draw a breath.

"Mother," Brand said.

"Brand," she said with a nod. "Worth." Her oldest son didn't meet her gaze. Up close he looked even older and in poor health. It broke her heart.

"Any news on Cyrus?" Pepper asked of her grandson.

"The same," Brand said, the pain evident in his expression. He glanced around the lodge. "The place hasn't changed." His gaze settled on her again. "Neither have you." He didn't make that sound like a good thing.

Enid appeared, giving them all a start and making Brand smile to himself.

"I suppose you want me to show them to their rooms," Enid said.

"I can do it." Virginia took hold of Brand's arm. "But maybe Enid could get them something to drink before dinner."

Enid shot Pepper a look that said she didn't take orders from Virginia especially with Virginia talking as if she wasn't even in the room.

"I think that is a wonderful idea, Virginia. I'll help

Enid and meet you all back down here in the parlor before dinner."

Enid turned on her heel and with a huff took off for the kitchen.

"She *really* hasn't changed," Brand said, sounding amused.

Virginia snorted. "I don't know why you haven't fired her a long time ago, Mother."

Pepper watched the housekeeper disappear down the hall. "Oh, I suspect Enid will die here."

Virginia led her brothers up the stairs and Pepper listened to the three of them whispering among themselves, joining ranks against the enemy. And she knew only too well who the enemy was.

CORDELL DIDN'T HAVE TO CALL his grandmother about tickets to the gala.

When Raine checked her cell phone as they left the Ambersons, there was a message from Marias that her CBA had sent her something.

Raine felt her stomach drop. "What now?"

"The message I got was that there will be two tickets for you at the door with your name on them for the Whitehorse Summer Gala. You've been invited to some exclusive party."

"What is it?" Cordell whispered, no doubt seeing Raine's expression.

"Apparently we're going to the dance," she said. "My benefactor left us tickets at the door. Anything else?" she asked Marias.

"Not that you want to hear," her friend and partner said. "I just keep wondering who's pulling your chain and why."

"Yeah. Me, too. Maybe they just want to see if I can dance."

Marias laughed. "Aren't they in for a thrill."

Raine hung up and looked over at Cordell. "What?" she asked, seeing his frown.

"At least if they're at the dance, then Lara is safe," he said.

She certainly hoped so. It felt as if time was running out. The last thing she wanted to be doing was going to some socialite dance in this wide spot in the road of a town while knowing Lara English was out there somewhere, scared and alone.

But she had to hold fast to her theory that the CBA wanted the truth to come out. As hard as it was for her to believe it was the same woman who'd kicked her over to the side of the floorboard as she'd gotten into the car sixteen years ago. The same woman who'd helped her husband abduct that terrified ten-year-old.

Suddenly a set of headlights flashed on. The next moment Raine heard the roar of an engine as what appeared to be a large truck ran right at them.

She saw Cordell swerve, the truck missing them by only inches as it sped past, and they crashed into the bushes at the edge of the road, breaking through and dropping down a small hill to come to an abrupt stop just feet from a narrow creek and in a stand of cottonwoods.

"Are you all right?" Cordell cried.

All she could do was nod. She was shaking all over after almost being run down for the second time in two days.

He turned to look back. She did the same, but she could see nothing but darkness. She could only think that she'd almost died on the road that she'd been abducted from so many years before. Was that how this was supposed to end? She was to die here sixteen years ago and had cheated the grim reaper—but only until now.

"That was no accident," Cordell said. "That means the driver of that truck knows that we went by the Ambersons. They must have tipped him off. Or whoever they called about Emily tipped the driver off. The Ambersons were upset. Of course they would call someone to see if it was true about her abduction by Orville Cline and tell the person that we'd been by."

Raine felt his gaze on her.

"Are you sure you're all right?"

She was trembling, still shaken by the near accident and that horrible feeling that this was where she was meant to die.

Cordell unhooked his seat belt, then reached over, unhooked hers and pulled her to him. The night was dark as a cloak around them. "It's going to be okay," he whispered against her hair.

Raine drew back and looked up at him. "You are such a terrible liar."

He smiled, eyes crinkling in the faint glow of the

dash lights, and suddenly it was as if they were the only two people left in the world. She leaned into him, wanting desperately to believe him. The night and the cottonwoods closed around the warm cab of the pickup like a cocoon.

She looked into his dark eyes and willed him to kiss her. She wanted to forget everything for just a while, to lose herself in this man's strong arms.

As if in answer, he lowered his mouth to hers. She snuggled against him, relishing the heat of his mouth, his body. He pulled her closer. Her body melded into his as he deepened the kiss. His tongue brushed over her lips, the corner of her mouth.

Her nipples hardened against the thin sheer fabric of her bra. She swore she could hear the quickened beat of his heart in sync with her own.

She encircled his neck as he trailed kisses along her jawbone and down the column of her throat. A shiver of naked desire moved through her. Raine could feel her pulse throb under his touch, a primitive beat like drums in her ears.

A moan escaped her lips as she felt his fingers unbutton her shirt. His mouth dipped to the tops of her breasts. She arched against him, felt his thumb flick over her aching-hard nipple. She bit her lip to keep from crying out as his mouth rooted out her naked breast from the sheer fabric of her bra.

The windows steamed over even on the warm summer night. Raine lost herself to the sound of their combined frenzied breathing, the rocking of the pickup, the feel of Cordell's body as he cradled her to him.

Her release came with a cry of pleasure that echoed through the cab, followed shortly by Cordell's own. They clung to each other, naked, breathing still ragged.

"I didn't mean for that to happen," Cordell said after a few minutes. "At least not in the pickup."

Raine kissed him. "I did," she said as she reached for strewn clothing.

Her cell phone rang as she was pulling on her jeans. "Hello," she said, still sounding winded.

"You all right?" Marias asked. "You sound funny."

"I'm fine." She glanced over at Cordell. "More than fine. What's up?"

A beat of silence that sent her heart off again, then Marias asking, "Then you haven't seen the news?"

"Have they found Lara English?" Raine asked, hope filling her.

"Orville Cline," Marias said. "He walked away from a work release prison program yesterday morning in Deer Lodge and hasn't been seen since."

Chapter Ten

Pepper Winchester studied each of her adult children as Enid served supper.

None of the three looked in the least bit happy to be here. So why were they here?

She could understand Brand coming. His son was in the hospital in a coma. But then if he was so miserable here at the ranch, then why not stay in a motel in town?

He could have easily come to Whitehorse without seeing her—or setting foot on the ranch.

"So has it changed that much from when you were last here?" she asked into the weighty silence.

All three seemed to be startled out of their thoughts.

"What?" Worth said. He was large like his father but without the extraordinary good looks that the other Winchester men had inherited.

"The ranch," she explained. "I was wondering if you'd missed it."

She saw Brand's jaw tense. He looked back down at

the food on his plate, his fork suspended over a piece of dried-out roast beef.

Pepper felt oddly sad to see that he had missed the ranch. The sting of being sent away all those years ago was still there in his expression.

They'd all been so vocal about getting away from the ranch and her, but they'd never left. She'd assumed they'd been waiting for their share of the infamous Winchester fortune.

Now she saw, in at least one case, she'd been wrong.

"You missed the ranch?" The question was directed at Brand.

He put down his fork, clearly refusing to look at her. His anger when he finally spoke was edged with disappointment.

"What do you expect, Mother? That we wouldn't miss this place?"

Not her, but the ranch.

She glanced at Virginia, who merely looked confused by the conversation, then shifted her gaze to Worth.

"What does this ranch mean to you?"

Virginia frowned. Worth opened his mouth, then closed it before looking across the table at his brother.

"We *were* the ranch," Brand said through gritted teeth. "It was us. We lived and breathed this place from the time we could sit a horse."

Pepper remembered all of them, Brand, Worth, Angus and even Virginia, working the ranch—and complaining about it. Back in those days even Enid and Alfred saddled up to help with branding and moving cattle.

"Don't you remember the cattle drives?" Brand asked, finally looking at her. "I thought you actually enjoyed them."

She had. She felt tears well in her eyes and turned her attention to her plate as she reminded herself that one of these people at this table—or even all three—might have been in on their youngest brother's murder.

ACTING SHERIFF MCCALL Winchester had her hands full. Everyone was out looking for Lara English. Fortunately it was June and the warm weather was holding. If Lara was just hiding somewhere, she should be fine.

And if she wasn't... That was what had McCall worried, especially after she'd been advised that Orville Cline had escaped. The child molester had confessed to abducting and killing a ten-year-old girl just outside of Whitehorse sixteen years before.

McCall would have been about the same age as Emily when the girl was taken. So why hadn't she heard about it?

She made copies of Orville Cline's mug shot and called in the deputies and leaders of the volunteers on the search parties.

"Pass this around," she'd told her deputies when she'd given them photos of Orville Cline. "Make sure everyone is on the lookout for him."

The girl's disappearance had made her cancel dinner at her grandmother's as well as her talk with Raine

Chandler. It bothered her that Raine had apparently let both McCall's cousin and grandmother believe she was a reporter.

What that might have to do with Cyrus's attack she had no idea. Maybe nothing. Maybe it had been as cut-and-dried as Cordell believed. Or not.

Suspicion came with the job, McCall thought as she nodded for the deputy to send in another of the children. She'd commandeered a room in the large farmhouse where the children lived with their foster mother. The foster father was a long-haul truck driver and on the road.

McCall had wanted to talk to each of the children. She had a feeling that one of them might know more than they told their foster mother.

A moment later, a skinny boy who looked to be about twelve came in. The first thing she noticed was how nervous he appeared. According to her list, his name was Clarence.

"So what is it you'd like to tell me, Clarence?" she said, smiling.

He started to say something, but she stopped him.

"I know you saw something. Don't worry, it's just between you and me and you'll feel better if you tell me. You liked Lara, didn't you?"

He nodded and swallowed, before choking out the words, "It was the bogeyman. He took her."

McCall leaned back. "The bogeyman?"

He nodded excitedly. "I saw him when we were playing hide-and-seek."

"What did he look like?" she asked casually.

"He was really big. I'd seen him in the trees before."

"You say he was big? Fat or tall?"

"Tall and big and strong."

"What color was his hair?"

Clarence shook his head. "He always had his hood up."

"Did you see his eyes? Were they dark or light?"

He shook his head. "I didn't get that close because he saw me. If he finds out I told—"

"He won't. I promise. Did you happen to see what he was driving?"

The boy looked confused. "He wasn't drivin' nothin'. He was hiding in the trees."

"He must have had a vehicle, though, right? Maybe parked over behind the hotel."

Clarence frowned and looked down. When he raised his gaze, she saw that he'd thought of something. "I guess that old brown van could have been his."

McCall felt her heart beat a little faster. "Did you see it last night when you and Lara and the other kids were playing hide-and-seek?"

"I was the only one who saw it when it hit that guy." The moment he'd let the words out, she could tell he wanted to snatch them and stuff them back into his mouth. "I wasn't supposed to say anything about that."

"Who told you not to say anything?" McCall asked, though she could guess.

He looked toward the door.

"I'm sure your mother had a reason for telling you to keep it to yourself," she added.

"She didn't want no one knowin' we were outside playing that time of the night," Clarence said.

Understandable. So he'd seen the van being driven by the bogeyman hit Cyrus Winchester.

"And you didn't see Lara after that?" she asked.

He shook his head. "She probably ran away after seeing the bogeyman hit that guy."

McCall figured that was exactly what his mother had thought, as well.

She showed the boy Orville Cline's mug shot, but he only shook his head. Even though he couldn't identify Cline as the bogeyman, she had a bad feeling Orville was already in town.

"THERE ISN'T ANYTHING ELSE we can do tonight," Cordell said as he shifted the pickup into four-wheel drive and drove down the creek to a spot where he could get back on the road above them.

Raine knew he was right. She was sure that the person who'd just run them off the road was more concerned with them than Lara. If Lara survived tonight she should be safe until after the Whitehorse Summer Gala tomorrow night.

Unless, of course, you added Orville Cline into the mix.

She told herself that something was going on between him and the couple who'd abducted her sixteen years ago.

Raine could only hope it was a falling out and not some kind of deal.

But as Cordell said, there was nothing she could do about it tonight. Who knew where Lara might be hidden. With all the old abandoned farmhouses and sheds around she could be anywhere.

All Raine could do was pray that Lara was still all right. She had to believe that whoever had gotten here would finally make contact tomorrow night at the dance.

They drove over to the hospital to visit his brother. Cyrus's condition hadn't changed. Raine could see the toll this was taking on Cordell and wished there was something she could do. Finding the person who'd done this was the only thing she could do. Tomorrow night at the dance, she promised herself. Someone would contact her. She had to believe that.

"Are you all right?" she asked Cordell as they left the hospital.

"Every hour, every day, that he doesn't wake up…" He took off his Stetson and raked a hand through his hair. "I keep telling myself that Cyrus is strong and no one has more determination. If anyone can come back from this it's him."

Raine took his hand as they walked out to his brother's pickup.

"Let's get something to eat. No way am I going

back out to the ranch. Want to take our chances at a motel?"

She nodded and squeezed his hand. They needed each other. She didn't kid herself that their lovemaking earlier had been anything more than that. But they had made love, tenderly and sweetly, and just the thought of being in his arms again warded off the chill of their circumstances for a while.

Cordell pulled into the drive-thru at the Dairy Queen and ordered them dinner, then drove to a motel on Highway 2. They ate sitting in the middle of the bed, eating and talking about anything but what was going on right now.

He told her about growing up on ranches, moving from one ranch to another as the jobs changed with his father and brother. Raine told him about growing up in North Dakota, fishing with her adopted father.

They watched the late news. Nothing new about Lara. Also no sign of Orville Cline, but law enforcement officers across the state were looking for him.

They showered together, then made love, lying afterward spent in each other's arms, and fell asleep comforting each other.

CORDELL WOKE TO FIND the bed beside him empty. He sat up with a start. Raine stood silhouetted against the open curtains of the window. Star and moonlight glittered around her.

He could see that she was hugging herself, staring

out at the night. He could well imagine her thoughts. Lara was never far from his.

Rising from the bed, he stepped up behind her to wrap his arms around her and look out into the night. She leaned back into him with a sigh and he felt the intimacy of this moment more strongly than even their lovemaking.

She turned in his arms to look up at him. "I don't know what I would have done without you and if it hadn't been for your brother..."

He kissed her gently.

"Do you believe in fate?"

Cordell smiled at that. She sounded like his brother. Even under the circumstances, Cyrus would have believed this was meant to happen. Cordell couldn't accept that. "I don't know why this has happened but I'm glad that you're safe."

She smiled and closed the curtains, letting him lead her back to bed. They lay side by side, both staring up at the ceiling.

"Who was she, the woman who hurt you?" Raine asked, turning to lean on an elbow to study him in the dim light of the motel room.

"Who said..." His voice trailed off as he met her gaze. "My ex-wife."

Raine nodded. "She broke your heart."

He smiled at that. "Let's just say she made me gun-shy when it comes to trusting women."

"I've noticed." She pushed a lock of his hair back from his forehead. "How long has it been?"

"Four years."

She let out a low whistle. "She really must have done a number on you."

He nodded and dragged his gaze away. "She wasn't who I thought she was."

Raine lay back again to look up at the ceiling. "Neither am I."

"You're Raine Chandler," he said, pushing himself up on an elbow to gaze into her wonderful face. "One of the strongest, most determined women I've ever met."

She smiled at that. "I don't feel very strong right now."

"You came back here even though you had to have suspected it was a trap," he said.

"As corny as it sounds, I wanted closure. I thought if I could get justice, as well, then…" She shook her head. "Now I couldn't quit if I wanted to."

No, and neither could he.

"What will you do when we find the person who hit your brother?" she asked, looking concerned.

Cordell shook his head. "If you're asking me if I will want to kill him, hell, yes. Will I? No."

"It will be enough for you to just turn him over to the sheriff?" she asked, surprised.

"It will have to be. I don't take the law into my own hands."

She said nothing.

"Raine? Is there something you're planning to do that I should know about?"

She met his gaze. "What if I was planning to kill the person responsible for Emily Frank's abduction?"

"I wouldn't blame you if you wanted to."

"But you wouldn't try to stop me."

He studied her for a long while before he said, "No."

She looped her arms around his neck and pulled him down to her. The kiss was filled with passion and heat. He felt the fire catch flame inside him. This time their lovemaking was fierce.

They weren't so different, the two of them, Cordell thought later as they lay spent in each other's arms. Both of them were afraid to trust, especially when it came to the opposite sex. And both of them wanted justice but could easily take vengeance.

He feared that after tomorrow night there would be no going back for either of them.

Chapter Eleven

The next evening Cordell looked up and saw Raine standing at the top of the stairs at the ranch lodge. His breath rushed out of him. She was beautiful. The gown his grandmother had given her fit like a glove, running over her curves like flowing water.

She hesitated, looking shy. But as their eyes met, she smiled and came down the stairs to take his outstretched hand.

"Wow," he said as he closed her hand in his. Something was changing between them. He could feel himself falling for this woman and it scared the hell out of him. With a start, he noticed she was wearing a tiny silver horse pin—the same one she'd been wearing the day she was abducted.

"You look beautiful," his grandmother said to Raine. She looked older and Cordell had picked up on the tension on the ranch with his father and aunt and uncle under the same roof.

"And you look very handsome," she said to him and reached out to touch his cheek. It was the most loving she'd ever been to him and it surprised him. "You look lovely together."

Raine looked away as if embarrassed. Or maybe, like him, for a moment she'd forgotten why they were dressed like this.

Cordell hoped her embarrassment wasn't because they weren't really together, not a couple, no matter how much Enid and his grandmother suspected they were. This was about catching monsters. He didn't doubt that Raine would hightail it back to California once it was over.

They didn't say much on the ride into town. For Cordell, the gravity of this evening had set in. Raine seemed lost in her own thoughts.

The moon came up, a huge golden orb that climbed up over the horizon into a vast sky studded with glittering stars. A warm breeze sighed among the leaves of the trees along the street as they parked outside the large old school where the dance was being held.

"You're sure about this?" he asked her as he cut the engine. Silence fell over them, the warm summer night making the inside of the pickup cab intimate. Cordell wanted to hang on to this moment, sitting here with Raine. It felt like a high-school date, both of them nervous and expectant. And for a moment he could pretend that was all this was.

DINNER COULD HAVE been much worse, Pepper Winchester thought halfway through the meal, although she couldn't imagine how.

The food was Enid's usual tasteless fare, Virginia hit the wine hard right away and her sons were more morose than ever.

She was counting down the minutes, hoping to put this meal and this night behind her when Brand tossed down his napkin before dessert was served and demanded, "What is it you want from us, Mother?"

"I don't want any—"

"She thinks one of us is responsible for Trace's death," Virginia spat out, sloshing her glass of wine as she put it down. "And she thinks one of her grandchildren saw the whole thing from the third-floor room."

That definitely answered the question of whether or not Virginia had done some eavesdropping of her own, Pepper thought.

"Well?" Brand demanded. "Is that true?"

There seemed no reason to deny it.

"You think one of us *killed* our own brother?" Brand was on his feet now, his face twisted in anger. "Have you lost your mind?"

Enid appeared then in her usual fashion—sneaking up on them. "Does this mean you won't be having dessert?"

"I'll have dessert," Virginia said, refilling her wineglass.

Pepper waved Enid back into the kitchen. "I have reason to believe that someone in this household conspired with the killer to have Trace murdered within sight of the lodge, yes."

"Someone in this household?" Worth asked.

"Don't you mean someone in the family?" Brand snapped.

"I suspect it was a member of this family because if I'm right, one of my grandchildren saw the murder—and covered for that person."

Brand was shaking his head. "So that's what this invitation back to the ranch was about." His rueful smile broke her heart. "I should have known. But for a moment there, I thought maybe, just maybe, you had changed. That you regretted what you did all those years ago. That you wanted to make amends. Or at least bring your family together to say goodbye."

His gaze bored into her and she felt his disappointment in her like a knife to the heart.

"Brand—"

"Don't, Mother. You want to know who killed your beloved son? You did. If one of us conspired with a killer to get rid of Trace, then you have only yourself to blame for pitting us against him." With that he stormed out of the dining room.

In the silence that dropped like a wet blanket over them, Enid appeared with a chocolate cake. She set it down in front of Virginia, along with a knife. Before Enid could turn to leave, Virginia picked up the knife and looked at the only other brother left at the table.

"Worth, are you going to have some cake with me?" Virginia asked. "It has to be better than dinner was."

"Sure," Worth said, his gaze going to his mother's.

Pepper felt a chill snake up her spine at the look in her son's eyes. As Virginia cut the cake, she watched her, realizing that either of these two could have been behind Trace's death.

But then they weren't the only ones at the table who were capable of murder, she thought as Virginia handed her a piece of cake.

"Who says you can't have your cake and eat it, too?" Virginia said with a laugh. "Isn't that right, Mother?"

THIS WAS IT, RAINE THOUGHT as Cordell parked the pickup. She could feel it. "They'll be here tonight," she said as she watched a group of laughing couples enter the building for the Whitehorse Summer Gala.

Music escaped as the front door of the school opened and died just as quickly as the huge doors closed.

She hoped this wasn't a mistake. All those people inside the school, all the noise... How would they find her? Or her find them.

But in her heart, she believed she would recognize the couple when she saw them. And if all else failed, recognize their voices. Some things she remembered only too well.

Still she felt torn, feeling they should be out looking for Lara instead, even though she knew their chances were next to impossible of finding the girl without help.

She met Cordell's dark gaze. What a gorgeous man both inside and out. She'd come to trust him, trust him with her life—and her secrets. That said more for his character than his good looks.

At his gentle, caring expression, she felt her heart kick up a beat.

"Raine, I just want to say—"

"I know," she said quickly, afraid of what he was going to say. They'd grown close too quickly. She didn't trust the feelings she had for him and certainly wouldn't trust his for her right now. This was too emotional for both of them. Maybe when this was over…

Raine refused to let her thoughts go there. "Let's do this."

He nodded, though looking disappointed she hadn't let him say what was on his mind, and reached for his door handle.

Outside the pickup, the warm summer breeze caressed her skin. She looked up at the stars in the midnight-blue canopy overhead and breathed it in, memorizing all of it. The feel of the breeze, the smell of summer, the awareness of the man beside her, knowing this could be the last time.

Cordell took her hand and squeezed it as they started up the steps and Raine took one more look at the summer night—a night made for lovers—before he opened the door and they slipped inside.

As they walked in, Raine felt as if everyone turned to look at them. Cordell pulled her closer, his hand warm on her waist, as they worked slowly through the crowd gathered around the dance floor.

She took strength in his touch and tried to relax. The couple who'd abducted her were in this room. She could feel it more strongly than ever.

Groups of people stood around talking, drinking and eating the food that had been laid out along several tables. The school gymnasium was decorated as if for a prom with glittering lights and a dark blue backdrop.

The voices, laughter and music blended together in a din. How would she ever be able to distinguish any one voice?

Fear seized her. This had been a fool's errand. She and Cordell should be out looking for Lara—not here at a dance.

As if seeing her panic, Cordell whispered next to her ear, "If they're here, they aren't with Lara."

She nodded. Lara was safe. At least until the dance was over.

They worked their way around the large room, picking up bits of conversations, looking for one couple, listening for a voice she recognized. After they'd made the loop twice, Cordell asked with a slight bow, "May I have this dance?"

Raine took his hand and let him lead her onto the dance floor. The band was playing a slow song. She laid her head on his shoulder and pretended they were merely a man and a woman dancing on a warm summer night.

But being in Cordell's arms sent her senses soaring. She loved the smell of him, the feel of him, and when he danced them into a dim corner, the taste of him as he kissed her.

He pulled back to look in her face. His gaze caressed her face, then settled on her lips an instant before he lowered his mouth to hers again. She melted into his embrace, into the kiss, and then he was dancing her back into the crowd, holding her closer as if they really were lovers.

Raine closed her eyes, wishing they had grown up in this town, been high-school sweethearts who'd settled on the ranch and went every year to the Whitehorse Summer Gala dance.

But instead she'd been abducted on the edge of this town and Cordell had been exiled from the ranch and his brother Cyrus now lay in a coma because of what had happened all those years before.

Earlier, she'd heard Cordell on the phone with the hospital. His twin's condition hadn't changed. She reminded herself that he was only helping her to get the people who'd injured his brother and find Lara and save her from these monsters.

But it was good to remind herself what they were doing here tonight and not let desire or emotion make this more than it was.

"Are you all right?" he asked, looking worried. "If you're right, the person will contact you."

She smiled and nodded. The song ended. "I'm going to find the ladies' room." She started to step away, but he grabbed her hand.

"Hurry back."

Her smile broadened as she saw the concern in his expression. She nodded and he released her, but she could feel his gaze on her as she wound through the crowd and away from him.

She studied the faces she passed. How different her life would have been if she'd known these people all her life. If she and Cordell really had been high-school sweethearts and there wasn't a child molester about to kill a little girl if they didn't find her.

Suddenly she was blinded by regret and rage, disappointment and determination. Life had not been kind to her and yet she'd survived it all. She'd never thought about being happy. She'd just been glad to be alive, not to be hungry, to have a roof over her head and a job.

She'd asked little of life.

But tonight she yearned for more. She wanted Cordell. She wanted happily ever after. And yet she feared that wasn't the destiny that awaited her and hadn't from the moment that car pulled up beside her sixteen years ago.

The music drifted on the air, growing fainter as she finally found a ladies' restroom deep in the building without a line. This one was empty. Her heels echoed on the tile as she rushed to the sink.

Turning on the cold water, she cupped it in her hands and splashed it on her face to wash away the hot angry tears that flowed down her cheeks.

Her heart ached at the memory of being in Cordell's arms on the dance floor, the way he'd looked at her when she'd come out in the dress, that amazing kiss and the look in his eyes just moments ago—

She grabbed one of the cloth towels and began to dry her face. Her makeup was ruined, her eyes red and swollen, and she could practically hear the clock with Lara's name on it, ticking down the minutes.

She knew what had her so upset and felt guilty for it. All her thoughts should be with Lara. But she was falling for Cordell Winchester. Last night in the pickup and again in the motel, it had been about lust and comfort and the need not to be alone with their thoughts and fears.

Tonight, though, in his arms on the dance floor… She couldn't bear the feelings he'd evoked in her. And she'd seen something in his gaze—

At the sound of the bathroom door swinging open she hurriedly rushed to the end stall.

The voices of two women melded together as they came through the restroom door. Faint music swept in with them, then the door closed and everything grew quiet.

Raine leaned against the stall wall, her face feeling hot. She was tired, completely drained, both emotionally and mentally. She knew she couldn't trust her emotions and had to pull herself together.

She'd hoped by now that one of them would have made contact. She had to believe that her theory was right—even though by all appearances the person had only gotten her back here to kill her.

No, she told herself. It was the man who'd taken Lara and tried to run Raine down. Just like tonight with that huge truck that had run them off the road. It was the man. The woman had to be the one who Marias called

CBA and she would contact her. Why else leave tickets for the dance at the door for her and Cordell?

But as she stood, her back against the stall wall, she felt as if this was hopeless. She would go back out there and mill until it was over and pray that she spotted the couple. After that...

She didn't have a clue what to do after that. A stall door down the line creaked open, then closed and locked.

"I can't believe what Nancy Harper is wearing," the woman in a far stall said.

"Ghastly," the other woman said from somewhere over by the long row of sinks. She sounded as if she was standing at the mirrors no doubt checking her makeup.

The woman flushed the toilet, the door unlocking and opening. Raine heard the woman's heels on the tile floor as she joined the other woman.

Neither seemed to realize Raine was in the last stall at the end of the long line. She thought about flushing the toilet and letting them know they'd been caught gossiping and might have, if the woman at the mirror hadn't spoken again.

"Do you think you can talk Frank into coming over for a drink after the dance?"

Raine froze at the sound of the woman's voice.

"It's going to be awfully late."

"I know but I picked up a bottle of wine I think you and Frank will like."

"Honey, is everything all right with you and Bill?"

"Of course." She laughed, a laugh that sent a blade of ice up Raine's spine. "It's just that he'll be tired and I'll be all wound up and not wanting the night to end."

"Well, I can ask Frank…" Their voices started to trail off.

Raine could barely hear the other woman's reply her heart was pounding so hard. The woman's voice, the one who'd stayed by the sinks. That was her! That was the voice of the woman who'd helped abduct her sixteen years ago.

CORDELL HAD WATCHED RAINE head for a ladies' restroom in the far recesses of the building. Now he felt anxious as he waited for her to reappear. The crowd kept obstructing his view of the hallway just enough to set his nerves on edge.

For a while with Raine in his arms on the dance floor, he'd forgotten that someone had made certain that she was here tonight by seeing that they got an invitation. But he hadn't noticed anyone taking any particular interest in either of them.

Oh, there were always a few men who couldn't help but notice Raine. But he hadn't seen anyone watching them and no one had made contact.

He was beginning to wonder if all of this wasn't just a way to torment Raine. The dance was almost over. If this woman, the one Raine's friend Marias called CBA, had gone to all this trouble to get Raine to Whitehorse and to this dance, then what was she waiting for? Had the woman lost her nerve?

As his cell phone vibrated in his pocket, Cordell began to move in the direction Raine had gone. He pulled out his phone and checked caller ID.

He was jostled by the crowd and forced to step outside one of the open doors. Standing on a small landing in the darkness, he snapped open his phone.

"How did you get this number?" he asked, still watching the hallway Raine had disappeared down.

A woman's chuckle. "Didn't Raine tell you? I'm amazing." Marias quickly turned serious. "I've left a dozen messages on her cell. This couldn't wait."

Cordell felt his blood run cold as he listened. "What did you just say?"

RAINE QUICKLY BENT DOWN and looked under the stalls. She saw two pairs of women's high heels. A pair of bright red strappy sandals and a pair of classic black high heels.

She didn't know which ones belonged to CBA. As the outer door closed, Raine quickly stepped from the stall and hurried after them.

Several more women were coming in as she reached the door and she had to wait as they passed before she could exit. By then, the two women had dissolved into the crowd.

She looked around frantically for Cordell, then at the array of shoes on the dance floor. She'd never find the woman before the dance ended and all she had was a name: Bill. There must be dozens of Bills in this town.

Raine moved along the edge of the crowd as quickly

as she could, searching for Cordell and the woman with the strappy red heels. There were too many black heels on the floor. She'd never find that woman.

As she passed an open door, she felt the cool summer night air beyond the darkness and wondered if Cordell had stepped out for some fresh air.

"Raine."

At the sound of her name, she turned back to step out into the dark. She blinked, trying to get her eyes to adjust, and saw no one. Had she just imagined someone calling her name?

She turned to look back into the huge glittering room. That was when she saw Cordell across the dance floor. He'd just stepped in from outside. He appeared to be searching for her, his cell phone to his ear. But it was his expression that turned her blood to ice.

There was a sound like the scrape of a shoe sole on the concrete behind her as she started to go back inside hoping she could reach Cordell before she lost him again in the crowd.

She was grabbed from behind. The cloth clamped over her mouth brought it all back. She was ten again on a dirt road in a strange place and terrified of what was about to happen to her. Only this time, she knew.

CORDELL DIDN'T THINK he'd heard Marias correctly over the music and the din.

"Orville Cline was sighted yesterday—just miles from Whitehorse. Do I have to tell you where he's headed?"

Cordell stepped back into the gym and began to push his way through the crowd in the direction Raine had gone. "You think he's the one who got Raine up here."

"Don't you?"

"He couldn't have done it alone. The van that tried to run her over, the tickets for this dance, the map. Raine is positive it's the woman—"

"Don't you get it? Raine needs to believe that. I'm catching the next plane out of here—"

"No, she needs you there in case she gets any more messages and there is nothing you can do here," Cordell said as he hurried down the hallway, the restroom door in sight. "I'll have Raine call you."

He reached the door, slammed it open. Several women at the sinks jumped, startled by his abrupt entrance— and the fact that a man had just burst into the women's restroom.

"Raine?" No answer. *"Raine?"* He bent to check under the stalls. Only one pair of heels, the wrong ones.

He turned and rushed out, his gaze frantically searching the crowd. No Raine. Cordell told himself not to panic. She was here somewhere. The dance had begun to thin out as the band wound down for the last song.

Raine, where the hell are you?

He bumped into a man, registering the man's conversation as he did.

"Don't be ridiculous, Adele," the man was saying.

Cordell's gaze went to the woman as he mumbled, "Excuse me," to the man. The man had backed her into a corner. She had tears in her eyes, her lipstick was smudged as if he'd just kissed her hard on the mouth.

The crowd didn't move and for a moment Cordell was unable to move, either. Next to him the man took the drink the woman was holding. "Are you trying to get me drunk, Adele?" He tilted his face toward her, moving in closer, dropping his voice as he gripped her jaw in his large hand. "Do you really think that will keep me home tonight?"

Cordell heard the anger in the man's words and saw fear in the woman's face—or was that open defiance? The crowd moved but Cordell stood rooted to the floor. What had stopped him cold was the hand gripping the woman's jaw—and the scar on the man's hand.

The bite mark was a perfect child-size half moon.

Chapter Twelve

"When was the last time you saw her?" Sheriff McCall Winchester asked.

Cordell rubbed a hand over his face. "No more than thirty minutes ago. I called you as soon as I found her pin out on the steps by one of the open doors."

They were sitting across from the school and had been watching everyone who came out of the building. No sign of Raine.

McCall picked up the tiny silver plated horse pin. "You think she dropped this on purpose?"

He nodded. "I knew the moment I saw it on the outside step glittering in the moonlight."

The sheriff eyed him. "Sorry, what is the significance of the pin?"

"She was wearing it when she was abducted here sixteen years ago."

"Abducted?" McCall sighed. "I think you'd better start at the beginning." She listened, taking notes only when necessary, as he told her about Emily Frank.

It was only after he'd finished that she demanded to

know why he hadn't come to her the moment he'd heard about Lara English being abducted.

"Raine said he would kill Lara if we did."

"Raine?" So that was the way it was, McCall thought, hearing the way he said the woman's name revealed just how involved his cousin was with her.

"But you called me now."

He gave her a tortured look. "I didn't know what else to do, especially since Orville Cline has escaped."

McCall nodded. "So we don't know who has Lara or Raine."

"But I do know who took Raine sixteen years ago." He told her about the bite scar. "I followed him to his car and got his license plate number." He handed her the gala napkin he'd written it down on. "I would have followed him and his wife home but I had to find Raine."

"And when you didn't, you found the pin and called me." She looked at the local license plate number. It wouldn't take long to run it. "You realize a scar on the man's hand isn't enough proof to arrest him."

"No, you need Raine to identify him. That's why we have to be careful. If Raine is right and his wife is the one who got her here…"

"What are you suggesting?"

"If this man took Lara English, then he will lead us to her."

"*Us?*" McCall said.

"I know you don't have the law enforcement officers to watch his house 24/7."

It was true.

"But I'm going to be watching him. I'll let you know the moment he makes a move."

McCall chewed on her cheek for a moment. "If you saw the man with the bite scar after Raine vanished…"

"He could have hidden her somewhere and returned to the dance. Or Orville might have her."

McCall didn't like the sound of that. "But why take Raine?"

"She was the only one who got away," Cordell said.

"I suppose it could be that simple." She ran the plate number and felt her pulse take off like a wild stallion.

The name Bill and Adele Beaumont came up on the screen.

"Do you know them?" Cordell asked, glancing over at the screen.

"Yeah," McCall said. "They own half the town."

"Raine said they would be above suspicion."

"So far the only thing you have against them is that they were at the dance tonight, they are prominent citizens and Bill has a scar which could be from a human bite—but may not be," McCall said.

"I also know that he's rough with his wife," Cordell said. "What about matching the bite scar with Raine's teeth prints? I realize she isn't ten anymore but I thought bite marks were like fingerprints, no two exactly alike?"

"Even if the crime lab could match Raine's bite with that of the marks on Bill Beaumont's scar, that doesn't prove that he abducted her. It would be hard to even prove that Raine is Emily Frank."

Cordell groaned. Clearly, he hadn't thought of that. "There has to be something we can do. Raine said the man who took Lara will keep her alive until tonight. If he thinks the sheriff is suspicious of him…"

McCall had to agree. Moving on Bill Beaumont if he was guilty would only cause him to get rid of the girl and Raine—if he had them both and if he hadn't already killed them.

"Okay, I'll put you on surveillance on the Beaumonts," McCall said, realizing she had little choice. She couldn't trust that if she used one of her deputies, it might get leaked to the Beaumonts. No one in this town would believe Bill was a child molester. Everyone would be ready to protect the local family against some weird-dressed California private investigator here stirring up things—and even more so against a Winchester.

"But the minute anyone makes a move, you call me. Don't you go playing Lone Ranger on me, cuz," she said.

"You got it." He reached for the door handle. "Raine's tough. She's gotten through a lot."

McCall nodded but knew he was just trying to convince himself because the fool had fallen in love with the woman and he couldn't bear the thought of her being with some sick monster. McCall couldn't, either.

If Cordell was right and Bill Beaumont had abducted Raine again, then he couldn't have taken her far. After she left her cousin, she began to search the area around the school, looking for an old house or shed, somewhere he could stash her.

If whoever grabbed her had seen that she got tickets to the gala, then he would have made prior arrangements.

As McCall drove around the area behind the school, she called her mother. "What do you know about Bill and Adele Beaumont?"

Most people when asked something like that would respond, "Why do you ask?"

Not Ruby. Her trade was gossip, she served it up with every order she delivered at the diner. It made up for the bad tips days.

She heard her mother take a long drag on her cigarette, turn down the television as she exhaled and ask, "Beaumont? Are they squabblin' again? I'm not surprised."

"Why do you say that?" McCall asked.

"You ever meet Bill, talk to him for two seconds, and you can see what a chauvinist he is. He's a jackass or worse."

"Worse?"

Ruby sighed. "Look how he treats Adele."

McCall pictured the slight petite woman. Every time she'd seen her, Adele was dressed to the T and made up as if she lived in a metropolitan area instead of Whitehorse, Montana.

"He doesn't seem to treat her too badly from what

I've seen," McCall said, thinking of the big new SUV Adele was driving.

"He has his thumb firmly on that woman. He says jump. She says, 'How high?'"

"Are you saying she's abused?"

"Depends on what you call abused. She lives in the nicest house in these parts, wears the best clothes money can buy, drives the nicest car, everyone in town treats her like she's royalty."

"And this is bad how?"

"I'll bet you this week's paycheck that once the two of them are alone inside that big house of theirs things are a whole lot different."

"What are you getting at?" McCall asked.

"Just a feeling I have," her mother said, usually not this noncommittal. "Let me tell you this. There are a handful of men who run this town. They all have coffee in the diner mornings, sit at the same table, even sit in the same chairs. Sometimes another man or two will join them. No one ever sits in Bill Beaumont's chair."

"Bill and Adele never had any kids," McCall remarked. "He would seem like a man who would want to leave his genes behind."

"They couldn't have any," Ruby said. "Her fault," she added before McCall could ask. "I heard he almost left her over it."

McCall shuddered. If Cordell was right, this could explain in some warped sick way why Adele went along with Bill's horrible "hobby."

"They could have adopted," McCall said.

"Bill? Are you serious? Why are you so curious about the Beaumonts?"

"I thought I saw them squabblin' outside the dance tonight." It wasn't exactly a lie. Cordell had seen them, even overheard them.

"He'll never leave her and he'll never let her leave him," Ruby said with authority. "He'd have to give her half his money. But I'll bet he makes her pay dearly for what she gets out of this marriage."

CORDELL SAT PARKED down the street under a large weeping willow tree and watched Bill Beaumont's house.

He and his wife, Adele, hadn't come home alone. Another couple had followed them from the dance and were now inside.

He could see the lights through the sheer drapes, catch glimpses of people moving around inside the house. He glanced at his watch anxiously.

Raine had been gone now for almost two hours. He wouldn't let himself think about what could have happened to her in that length of time.

She was smart and capable and stronger than any woman he'd ever met. He had to believe that she was all right and would survive this, just as she'd survived being a foster child and her abduction at ten.

His cell phone rang, startling him out of his thoughts. He checked the caller ID. Marias.

"I told you I would call you when I heard something," he said into the phone.

"Another message just came through from the CBA." Marias took a breath and let it out. In that breath he heard her anger—and her fear. "This one, though, is for you. It says, 'Unless you want to end up like your brother and your girlfriend, back off. This has nothing to do with you.'"

"Like hell," Cordell said under his breath and hung up.

Just after 2:00 a.m., the couple who'd been visiting the Beaumont house walked out to their car. They appeared to be arguing, their voices carrying on the cool night air.

Cordell whirred down his window.

"I'm telling you she didn't want to be left alone with him," the woman said.

"It's two in the damned morning, Theresa. You want to go back in there and babysit her, fine, but I'm going home and going to bed."

The woman looked toward the house, clearly conflicted. "She's afraid of him."

The man scoffed as he opened his car door. "Yeah, Bill's a real scary guy," he said sarcastically.

The woman seemed to make up her mind. She opened her car door, glanced back at the house once more, then joined her husband, closing the door behind her.

Brake lights flashed, the engine turned over. Inside the house someone moved behind the sheer drapes as the couple drove away down the street.

Cordell glanced at his watch again twenty minutes later. The dial glowed. He could feel the minutes ticking by. What if he was wrong? What if the real monster was with Raine right now?

There were two vehicles parked in front of the Beaumont home. A pickup and a large SUV. When the porch light snapped off, Cordell felt his heart drop. Was it possible Bill Beaumont wasn't going anywhere tonight?

He couldn't bear the thought of Raine in some horrible place any longer. He started to open his door, not sure what he planned to do, but he was going up to that house and if he had to, he would beat the truth out of Bill Beaumont.

Through a crack in the drapes he could see movement. Someone was pacing back and forth and appeared to be having a heated argument.

He eased his door open and climbed out. Working his way through the shadowed darkness of the trees, he neared the house. He could hear muted voices, the man's more strident, the woman's meek.

Along the side of the house, he found an open window and eased it open wider. He could hear snatches of the argument.

Bill was worked up, yelling at his wife, who seemed to be trying to console him.

Cordell was about to go in the window when he realized everything had gone silent.

At the sound of the front door opening and slamming shut, he rushed to the edge of the house. Bill was climbing into his pickup truck. An instant later, the engine turned over and Bill threw the truck into Reverse and roared out of the yard, the tires spitting gravel.

Cordell waited a moment to make sure he wasn't seen before sprinting to his brother's pickup and following.

For the first time all night, he felt hope that he might actually find Raine before it was too late.

Out of the corner of his eye, he saw the drapes part on the front window of the Beaumont house. He had only an impression of a woman watching him as he drove off.

"SEE IF YOU CAN FIND any connection between Bill Beaumont and Orville Cline," McCall said into the phone.

"The child molester in Montana State Prison?"

"There have to be phone records or even visits." Would Beaumont be so stupid as to visit Orville Cline in prison?

McCall hung up and glanced at the clock. She hadn't heard from Cordell and could only assume that Bill hadn't left his house.

She'd known Bill since she was a kid. He was one of those do-gooders, as her mother Ruby called him.

"A terrible tipper though," her mother had always been quick to point out. "He and his cronies come in to the café, drink gallons of coffee for hours and leave a measly tip for one cup of coffee. His wife is worse. You'd think they were headed for the poor farm the way they pinch pennies. That's the rich for you."

Ruby Bates Winchester measured everyone in town by how generous they were with her at the diner. McCall wondered if it didn't have more to do with the service they got from her mother than how tight they were with their money.

For a moment, she thought about her mother and how much she'd changed since she started dating Red Harper. McCall had never seen her mother truly happy before and now that she was, it was a beautiful thing. She hoped it lasted.

Her mother had taken the news about her husband Trace Winchester's murder twenty-seven years ago in her stride. At least on the surface.

But McCall had happened to see her mother at the cemetery one evening just before dark. Ruby was sitting beside the huge ornate tombstone Trace's mother, Pepper, had insisted on. But Ruby had won the battle about where her husband and the father of her daughter would be buried.

"I want him in town so I can visit him," she'd told Pepper on one of the few occasions the two women actually spoke to each other.

Pepper had wanted Trace buried in the family plot on the ranch. It was one of the few times her grandmother have given in.

McCall had been touched by Pepper's generosity in letting Ruby have this small victory, especially since Pepper had tried so hard when Trace was alive to split them up.

McCall told herself that was all water under the bridge. Her father was dead and buried. Any doubts she had about who had killed him, she'd tried to bury with her father.

That evening, though, when she'd seen her mother sitting on Trace's grave in the cemetery, McCall had stopped and watched Ruby gently touching the grave-stone, talking to the husband she'd lost when she was pregnant with McCall.

Maybe they would all find peace, she'd thought that night. Someday.

It was one reason she'd agreed to have her wedding with Luke at Winchester Ranch. Even with the animos-ity between her mother and grandmother. She hoped the two could call a truce—at least until the wedding and reception were over.

McCall had reluctantly accepted her grandmother's generous offer to host the wedding at Winchester Ranch on Christmas. She knew Ruby was excited about finally setting foot on the ranch after all these years.

McCall just hoped the wedding went off without any bloodshed. With the Winchesters, you just never knew.

Her phone rang. She picked it up thinking it would be Cordell with an update on what was or wasn't hap-pening at the Beaumont house. She feared letting him run surveillance might be a mistake.

But the call was from one of her deputies letting her know that they hadn't found Lara English and were calling it a night. They'd begin again in the morning.

"Thanks, Nick. Please thank the volunteers and make sure everyone gets home safely." McCall had spent hours earlier as part of the search party and knew how emotionally draining it could be when you might be looking for a body instead of a little girl.

Unable to wait any longer, McCall called Cordell's cell. The phone rang four times before going to voice mail.

She frowned and hung up, her anxiety growing. She waited a few minutes and tried the number again. Still no answer.

Grabbing her hat and keys, she headed for her patrol SUV.

Chapter Thirteen

McCall drove by the Beaumont house and didn't see Cordell's pickup anywhere on the street—nor any sign of him. Didn't mean that he wasn't still watching the house, she told herself.

Before driving over here, she'd gone out to her cabin on the Milk River and changed into dark jeans, boots, a dark long-sleeved T-shirt. She'd left the patrol SUV and took her pickup instead.

Now she parked and walked down the deserted street watching for any sign of her cousin. As she neared the Beaumont house she caught a glimpse of Adele through the sheer drapes at the front window.

Like McCall, she'd changed her clothing since the dance and now wore jeans and a shirt. She seemed to be pacing. McCall slowed at the edge of the yard and stepped into the shadows of the trees that lined the property as Adele suddenly froze, then hurriedly picked up her cell phone. She glanced at caller ID, then took the call.

McCall moved closer, never taking her eyes off the

woman. Adele looked upset and Bill's pickup wasn't in the driveway. Could be in the garage.

Peeking in the garage, McCall found it empty. No Bill. No Cordell. She didn't even have to venture a guess where Cordell had gone. Wherever Bill had headed. She silently cursed him for not following her orders.

As she moved away from the garage, she saw that Adele was still on the phone. But if the woman had been upset before the call, now she seemed to be in a panic. She moved one way then another, appearing frantic as if looking for something.

McCall saw her snatch up her purse from where she must have dropped it earlier and, snapping the phone shut, headed for the door.

Ducking back into the shrubbery and trees, the sheriff stayed hidden as Adele, wearing a black jean jacket, got into her car and backed out. The headlights flashed over McCall, then darkness closed in again.

As she hurried to her truck, McCall wondered where Adele was headed this time of night and what had her so upset. Who had been on the phone? Bill? And if so, where was Cordell?

CORDELL HAD KNOWN that tailing anyone in a town this small was tough. At this time of the night with no traffic at all, and Bill Beaumont looking for a tail, it was nearly impossible.

His heart was racing at the thought that the man driving the truck in front of him was about to take him straight to Lara English and Raine.

But where was Orville Cline? He and Beaumont had to be in this together.

He thought about the fight he'd overheard between the Beaumonts. By her tone, Cordell knew Adele had been pleading with her husband, but Cordell hadn't been close enough to hear what she was saying. But earlier Bill had accused her of trying to keep him home tonight.

Apparently Adele Beaumont had lost the argument since her husband had left the house.

Cordell drove up a few blocks and pulled over, cutting his lights as Beaumont continued down the main drag, then turned right through the underpass. From where he'd pulled over, Cordell could see the street on the other side of the underpass. Beaumont turned left.

Cordell went after him, through the underpass and up onto Highway 2. He saw no sign of taillights. He should have been able to see him, Beaumont didn't have that much of a lead. Cordell swore. Maybe he'd taken a right on Highway 191 and was headed for Canada.

But as he pulled out, he saw Beaumont's pickup parked in an empty dirt lot at the turnoff. He appeared to be on his cell phone.

Cordell drove past and pulled into the open-all-night Westside gas station. He got out, and watching Beaumont across the road, paid with his credit card and filled up his tank. Beaumont got off the phone. A few minutes after 3:00 a.m., a car came up the highway. The driver slowed, glancing over at Beaumont. As the car headed north, Beaumont fell in behind it.

Heart in his throat, Cordell climbed back into the pickup. His hands were shaking. He'd only gotten a glimpse of the man in the car—but it had been more than enough to know that the driver was Orville Cline.

Orville was now leading Bill Beaumont north out of Whitehorse.

McCALL GOT THE FIRST CALL just after she turned off the road. Keeping Adele Beaumont's SUV taillights in her view, she slowed and picked up. "Winchester."

"I'm following Beaumont north," Cordell said without preamble. "He just picked up Orville Cline."

McCall didn't waste her breath giving him hell for not calling her sooner. "Stay on them, but don't make a move against them. I mean it, Cordell. You call it in when they stop. Got that?"

She waited for a reply but realized she'd already lost him. She cursed under her breath. Adele wasn't headed north but south out of town. McCall had hoped that Raine and Lara were being held together. Now that didn't look as if it was the case.

Ahead Adele was turning off onto a side road. McCall followed slowly, not about to use her headlights or brakes and cause Adele to know she was being followed. The moon was bright enough that she could see the road well.

McCall knew this area south of town. There was an old farmhouse down in a hollow, the same hollow Adele's big SUV had just dropped into. She drove only a little farther up the road and pulled off far enough that her pickup couldn't be seen from the road.

When her cell vibrated again, she jumped and realized how tense she was. Everything about this had her on edge. Three civilians lives were at risk. Her first thought was to call in the troops, but she immediately changed her mind. She couldn't be sure who was waiting in that farmhouse and what they would do if backed into a corner.

She was on her own, she thought as she took the call.

"I got the warden up at the prison out of bed," Deputy Shane Corbett said. "He said to tell you that you are on his mud list for getting him up at this hour."

"I can live with that. What did you find out?"

"He had the information handy since every law enforcement officer in the northwest is looking for Orville Cline right now. He'd already checked on Cline's visitors, especially recent ones. Bill Beaumont wasn't one of them."

McCall had been hoping for a connection. Right now she had nothing against the Beaumonts except a scar and a suspicion—both flimsy at best.

"But Cline did have another visitor two days before he escaped," Shane was saying. "The two got into an argument and the visitor was asked to leave."

The sheriff couldn't hide her shock as Shane told her the name of the prisoner's visitor.

"Adele Beaumont visited Cline?"

"She was supposedly there to deliver some books as part of an inmate reading program Cline was involved in."

A cover. Her heart was beating so hard she could barely make out Shane's next words.

"Orville Cline was worked up good after that. The warden said he didn't think too much about it when he was told about the encounter. Now though..."

"Yeah," McCall said as she continued to follow the faint glow of taillights into no-man's-land. "I might need some backup. I'm going after Adele Beaumont right now. We're about fifteen miles south of town on Alkali Creek Road."

She heard Shane let out a breath.

"The Beaumonts may be involved in the abduction of Lara English," she told the deputy. "It's a long story, but one of their alleged victims got away sixteen years ago. She's back in town but has disappeared. Better call Luke and bring in the rest of the deputies. My cousin Cordell was watching the Beaumont house earlier tonight and is now following Bill Beaumont and Orville Cline. They are headed north out of town."

Shane swore under his breath. "Is there anyone who's not missing?"

"Don't do anything until I call," she said, afraid that if they all went in like gangbusters, it would jeopardize both Lara's and Raine's lives. "Just be ready."

"You got it," Shane said.

McCall checked her gun, grabbed another clip and

her shotgun, before stepping out into the summer night to begin walking across country toward the old Terringer place.

CORDELL SAW THE TWO VEHICLES in the distance turn off the highway onto a side dirt road that led back toward the Milk River.

He noted the way they slowed and knew they were waiting to see if the car they'd spotted behind them slowed, as well. He kept going, driving past, keeping his speed up. He could see them waiting and had to drive another five miles up the highway before the road turned and his taillights disappeared from view.

Hitting the brakes, he pulled over. For the past five miles, he'd been looking for other side roads that headed down to the river. There was one about two miles back. It wasn't ideal. He couldn't be sure it would take him in the direction he needed to go, but he could be sure that Cline and Beaumont would be watching the road they'd taken.

Turning out his headlights, he flipped a U-turn in the road and headed back to where he'd seen the other road. In the distance, he couldn't see any lights from the two vehicles and assumed they'd driven down into the river bottom. There must be some kind of old building down there. They sure as heck weren't going fishing at this time of the morning.

He had to believe that the two would lead him to Raine and Lara.

Taking the side road, he drove down until the dirt

track ended at the river and he saw that it was nothing more than a fishing access. He parked and checked his gun, then got another clip out of the glove box, before he sprinted south along a game trail that ran parallel to the river in the direction Cline and Beaumont had gone. Even in the moonlight it was hard to run along the uneven path.

But Cordell could feel the minutes slipping away. He had to get there in time.

LARA PULLED THE OLD blanket around her not sure what had awakened her. When she'd heard the door open, her only thought had been food. But she was also cold. Maybe the woman was bringing her dress back after washing it for her.

She reminded herself to thank the woman and not make her angry. But she was so tired and cold and hungry that it was hard to concentrate. She just hoped whoever was coming would bring her food and something to drink.

Too late Lara had realized she shouldn't have eaten all the food they brought the last time or drunk all the water. It had been hours now that her stomach had ached for something to eat.

Lara felt a gush of cold air as someone entered the room she was in. She shivered and sank deeper into the blanket wrapped around her.

As badly as she wanted food and water, she was filled with dread at seeing the people who had taken her again. She'd tried not to think about why they were keeping her here or what they wanted. But after all this time, she couldn't help but worry.

She caught the scent of perfume and the single beam of a flashlight, her dread deepening as she realized the woman had come alone. The woman set something down. A moment later the room was filled with light.

The lock scratched open and the door of the box swung out. Lara closed her eyes against the glare of the light, huddling in the blanket, shivering from more than the cold as she sensed the woman standing over her simply staring down at her.

"Little girl," the woman finally snapped. "Your new mommy is here."

Lara swallowed the lump in her throat and parted the blanket to peer up at her. Her new mommy?

The blanket was suddenly jerked away. Lara cowered, afraid the woman was going to hit her. Instead, all she did was stare at her for a long time before she said, "Stand up."

Lara did as she was told even though her legs threatened to fold on her. Weak and cold, she stood shivering, hugging herself.

"Put your arms down," the woman snapped.

She did. Then the woman did something that surprised her. She reached out and brushed a lock of her hair back from Lara's face.

Lara looked up at her expectantly. Maybe the woman wasn't going to hurt her. But she didn't seem to have brought her anything, either, no food, no water, nothing to wear, and she'd thrown the blanket in the corner of the rotting floor of the old house as if she no longer needed it.

For just an instant, there was something almost kind in the woman's eyes. Or was it regret?

"I'm hungry," Lara said and instantly wished she hadn't. She felt her heart begin to pound under her skinny chest as she saw the woman's expression change.

"You're just like all the others, aren't you? No matter what we do for you, it's just never quite enough."

"I'm not hungry," Lara said quickly. "I'm not."

The woman shook her head as she reached into the pocket of her jacket and drew out a knife.

"You're a bad girl. A very bad girl. Mommy is going to have to punish you."

Chapter Fourteen

"She's still alive?" The voice if not the words sent a cold blade of terror through Raine. It was the man who'd abducted her sixteen years before. She would never forget that voice.

"I'm not trying to do your dirty work for you again. The deal was I get her for you and you get me what I want. What you do with her is your business. I've done my part."

"You're sure it's her?" asked the man whose voice she recognized.

"I got her to town for you. If you don't believe it's her, have a look for yourself. But don't be questioning if I know what I'm doing, all right?"

"Sorry, Orville."

Raine froze as the beam of a flashlight flickered over the box she was in. She'd gotten the tape off but now left a piece loosely wrapped over her bare ankles. She hoped it would appear she was still bound, but she couldn't see her ankles well enough to know if it worked or not. She put her hands behind her and wrapped the tape as best she could on her wrists.

Raine had no plan, just a determination to survive. She thought of Cordell as she heard what sounded like a bolt being slid back on the top of the box. Earlier tonight Cordell had tried to tell her how he felt about her but she'd stopped him. She silently cursed herself for doing that. Now she might never hear those words.

The door swung open with a loud groan. She blinked as the light fell over her. Two men stood in the glow of the ambient light from the flashlight. One was tall, thin, his face angular and narrow giving her the impression of a fox. Orville Cline. She recognized him from his mug shot.

The other was handsome, square-shouldered, blue-eyed with a head of thick black hair. It was no wonder he'd gotten away with this for so long. Who would ever suspect a man who looked like that?

Sheer terror filled her. She'd told herself all these years that she didn't remember what either of her abductors had looked like. Their faces had been lost in the other memories, the ones she'd refused to let surface.

But the memory came back in a rush. It felt as if she'd been kicked in the stomach. She remembered him.

"Emily?" He stepped closer.

It took every ounce of her self-control to remain still as he knelt down beside her and, holding the flashlight in one hand, grabbed her jaw between his fingers to force her to look into his eyes.

She cringed, remembering his hands on her. Her mind went numb. She lay there unable to move, hardly able to breathe.

His eyes searched hers and then he laughed and let go of her. "Oh, yeah, you're Emily. My sweet Emily."

Anger stirred in her. Raine felt her heart begin to pound wildly as rage raced through her veins hot as lava. He was still kneeling in front of her, this horrible man. Last time he'd touched her, she'd been only a child, defenseless. But she would no longer be his victim. She felt her hands fist behind her. The past seemed to shed from her like snakeskin.

He rose as if seeing something in her gaze that warned him.

But he didn't know she was no longer bound. All she had to do was kick out at his ankles. She could be on her feet in an instant. She'd spent years studying martial arts for just this moment.

"Come on," Orville Cline said behind him. "I gave you what you wanted. Now you give me mine, Billy Boy. Take me to mine and then you can come back to your sweet Emily," Orville Cline said mockingly.

"I'm not going to tell you again that my name is Bill."

"Whatever you say, Billy Boy," Orville said, amusement in his voice.

Raine realized with a jolt what Bill-Billy-Boy had done. He'd made a deal with Orville and that deal was Lara English. She'd been wrong. She'd thought for sure it was the woman who'd gotten her here. Now she saw her error.

But where was the woman?

Realization came with a flash.

The woman was with Lara.

Raine knew that if she attacked the man now, she would be jeopardizing Lara's life. As furious as she was, she knew she could take him and would stand a decent chance of taking Orville Cline, as well.

But what if the woman was waiting for a call from Billy Boy?

Common sense won out over her fury. She lay perfectly still as he slammed the lid on the box and turned to leave.

He'd forgotten to slide the bolt!

Raine held her breath, praying he wouldn't remember as the beam of his flashlight headed for the stairs, Cline following him. She listened to their heavy tread on the stairs, then start across the floor upstairs.

She couldn't stand it a moment longer. As quietly as possible, she lifted the lid of the box and, stripping off the ripped tape from her wrists and ankles, she got to her feet in the pitch blackness. She felt dizzy and her legs were weak from being in such a cramped position for so long.

She realized it would have been folly to have tried to attack him. A mistake that would have gotten her killed—if she was lucky. She hated to think what he had planned for her.

Carefully she stepped out of the box into the pitch blackness. She recalled where the door to the room was and moved cautiously toward it. Beyond that was the bottom of the stairs. She was halfway up the stairs when

she heard the sound of footsteps coming back across
the floor toward the top of the stairs.

One of them was coming back.

LARA WONDERED WHAT THE woman was going to do
with the knife. She stared at the shiny blade in the glow
of the flashlight beam, hypnotized.

A whisper of a sound behind her new mommy with
the knife made her look toward the darkness. She caught
movement and for just a moment she thought it was the
man.

All hope that he'd brought her food and something to
drink evaporated as she saw that it was another woman
and the only thing she had in her hand was a gun. The
second woman put her finger to her lips for Lara to be
quiet.

Lara was always quiet. She brought her focus back to
the knife. Her new mommy had a grip on her wrist, her
nails biting into her flesh, but Lara didn't cry out. She
bit back on the pain the same way she did the fear.

Her stomach growled and her throat was so dry she
could barely swallow. She felt dizzy and weak and just
standing took all her energy.

Lara saw that the other woman was dressed in a
uniform. The woman again touched her fingers to her
lips and Lara nodded and felt tears fill her eyes. She
wondered if she should tell her new mommy.

As if sensing something wrong, her new mommy
looked up at her. "Don't you dare start blubbering."

Lara hurriedly shook her head and made a swipe at her tears with her dirty hand.

But the tears wouldn't stop. It was as if a dam had broken. Her body began to tremble, then shudder with the sobs.

"I told you—"

The slap came as no surprise to Lara. It rang out in the empty house like a gunshot as she tried desperately to quit crying, knowing that what was coming next would be much worse.

CORDELL SAW THE FLICKER of light through one of the glassless windows of the old house ahead. He slowed to catch his breath and scope out the scene.

There was a car and a pickup parked outside. As far as he could tell that meant that only Bill Beaumont and Orville Cline were inside the house.

Beside the car, he caught a small flash of light, then something glowed for a moment in the darkness. The smell of cigarette smoke drifted on the night breeze. Orville Cline leaned against the side of the car waiting.

Cordell moved cautiously around the other side of the house, the side by the river. No light now shone in the house. Had Bill come back out? Nearing the corner of the building, he peered around it.

Orville was still smoking over by his car. No one else was in sight. That had to mean Bill was still inside the house. With Raine and Lara?

Cordell backtracked to the first large glassless window opening and hoisted himself up onto the sill.

He knew he would be a perfect target against the moon-lit night and quickly lowered himself to the floor as soundlessly as possible.

The worn floorboards creaked under his weight as he took a step, then another as his eyes adjusted to the darkness inside the old abandoned house. As he moved deeper into the house, he saw light coming up from a stairway that led down to what must have been a partial basement.

That was where Raine and Lara had to be. The thought sent a shaft of fear through him as there was no sound coming from down there except for the heavy tread on the stairs.

Weapon ready, he moved toward the stair opening.

The board under his boot heel creaked loudly and he froze as a male voice yelled up from below, "I told you to wait. I just need to take care of something and then we'll go."

A sound outside, then the flicker of a flashlight beam as it headed this way. Cordell had a split second to make the decision whether to fire, kill Orville and then take care of Bill Beaumont in the basement.

He couldn't risk what Beaumont would do to Lara and Raine before he could get to them. He ducked around the corner into a small room as Orville Cline entered the house.

IN THE GLOW OF LANTERN LIGHT, McCall edged up behind Adele Beaumont. She was so filled with disgust that her heart was pounding. Lara huddled in the corner of the dirt floor, a filthy hand covering the red cheek that Adele had slapped.

Adele seemed to be alone. McCall made sure before she stepped closer. That was when she noticed the knife in the other woman's hand.

The girl had seen her and burst into tears no doubt with relief.

Just the sight of the girl huddled there naked, shivering from cold and fear, broke McCall's heart. She'd known Adele and Bill Beaumont, not well, but had seen them around for years. How could they do something like this?

She had never felt such fury. It was all she could do not to rush at the woman. She wanted to hurt her like she'd hurt Lara.

Timing it, McCall shoved the barrel of the pistol into Adele's back and knocked the knife out of the woman's hand.

"You touch that child again and I will blow your brains out," McCall said through gritted teeth.

She felt Adele freeze, then begin to cry. "I was trying to save her. I—"

McCall started to call in her location when Adele made a lunge for the knife.

She swung the gun, catching Adele across the side of the face. She howled as she fell over onto the dirt.

"Are you crazy?" Adele screamed. "I was trying to rescue—"

"Get up and take off your jacket."

"What?" Anger flared in Adele's gaze.

"Take off your jacket and give it to the girl. Now!"

Adele shoved herself up into a sitting position, glaring angrily. "I will sue the sheriff's department for everything it's worth. You have no idea what you've done. Your career is over. I will destroy you."

"Shut up." McCall snatched the jacket from Adele's fingers and tossed it to Lara. "Put that on, sweetie. Everything is going to be all right now."

"Where are this child's clothes?" she demanded of Adele, the weapon aimed at her heart.

"You're making a huge mistake, Sheriff," Adele said with venom. "You will live to regret this."

McCall looked down at her and felt her finger caress the trigger of the pistol. Why waste taxpayers' money with a trial or letting this woman live for years in prison or a mental hospital? What if Adele pulled strings, hired the best lawyer money could buy and got out one day to do this again?

She glanced over at Lara, who'd pulled on the jacket. "It's going to be all right." McCall smiled over at the girl, keeping an eye on Adele, the gun pointed at the woman's heart.

Lara took a shuddering breath and nodded, not looking all that sure.

McCall eased her finger off the trigger. It was the hardest thing she'd ever had to do. And she again started to make the call for backup.

Adele came flying at her with a piece of broken chair leg McCall now remembered seeing nearby. The blow knocked the gun from McCall's hand. It skittered across the dirt floor out of her reach.

Adele hit her again, knocking her to the floor. McCall got an arm up to ward off the next blow, but Adele was relentless. As McCall lunged for her gun, she saw Adele scoop up the knife from the floor.

McCall snatched up her weapon and swung around but too late. Adele had Lara and was holding the knife to her throat.

"Drop the gun, *Sheriff,* or you know what I'll do to this precious little girl, don't you?"

IN THE DARKNESS, Raine backed down the stairs as quickly as possible as a flashlight beam played on the steps above her. She'd just reached the bottom when she heard Bill stop, turn back and yell at Orville.

Like Bill, she'd heard the other set of footfalls on the wooden floor overhead. She'd hoped that it was Orville being impatient enough that Bill wouldn't come back down. Why was he anyway?

"What the hell is wrong with you?" It was Orville. She heard him come storming into the house.

Her mind raced. The other footfalls couldn't have been him then.

Bill had stopped at the top of the stairs. "I told you to wait out by the car."

"What do you think I was doing? Then I hear you yelling..."

Raine backed up, stumbled into something that teetered and threatened to topple over. She spun around and grabbed for a small wooden crate that someone had stood on end. She could barely make it out in what little light spilled down from the stairs from Bill's flashlight.

But as her hand closed on it and she heard the footsteps lumbering the rest of the way down the stairs, she hefted it up and pressed her back to the wall. There wasn't time to close the lid on the box, which meant that within just a few seconds Bill would shine his flashlight beam into the box and realize she was gone.

Not gone. Since there was no way she'd had time to leave this room. Which meant—

The flashlight beam flicked over the box.

"What the hell?!" Bill cried.

Behind him, Orville said, "What is it?"

Raine stepped around the edge of the wall and swung the crate with all her strength.

The sound of the wood splintering as it connected with her abductor's face couldn't drown out his scream. It surprised her that she took no pleasure in the sound.

His flashlight fell to the floor, the light cutting a swath through the empty room toward the far wall. As he reached for her, Raine kicked out at him, catching him in the knee.

He slammed into the wall next to him as the knee gave way.

But before she could strike again, she saw the gun and heard the click as he snapped off the safety and aimed the barrel at her heart.

"I should have killed you sixteen years ago."

CORDELL MOVED FAST. He had no idea what was happening down in the basement, but something was definitely happening.

He came up behind Orville Cline swiftly and jammed the gun into his back. "Downstairs," he ordered, forcing Orville ahead of him.

The basement was a partial one just as Cordell had thought. The ceiling was low, the air dank, the space dark and claustrophobic. He'd feared that the moment they reached the basement, Bill Beaumont would see them.

But Cordell couldn't take the chance that Beaumont would hurt Raine and Lara if he waited. He kept the gun in Orville Cline's back as he quickly assessed the situation.

No Lara. And Beaumont was holding a gun on Raine.

"Got a problem here," Orville said.

"Well, I'm about to end this problem," Beaumont said.

"I wouldn't do that," Cordell said.

Beaumont swung around in surprise, leading with the barrel of his gun. He got off a shot before Raine attacked him. That shot caught Orville Cline in the chest. He let out a grunt and started to fall forward.

Cordell shoved him out of the way, Orville crashed through an open doorway and into a coffinlike box, as Cordell scrambled to get to Raine. Raine and Beaumont were on the floor, fighting over Beaumont's gun.

Just as Cordell grabbed for the gun, Beaumont pulled

the trigger. Fire shot through Cordell's arm. Then he was knocked back, his gun wrested from him, and Beaumont had an arm locked around Raine's throat and the gun pointed at Cordell's head.

"Emily and I are leaving," Beaumont said, sounding winded. "If you follow us, I will kill her."

Cordell looked into Raine's eyes. One of them had started to swell where Beaumont must have hit her.

"Do as he says," Raine said. "I'll be all right." She was looking at his bleeding arm with concern.

"Listen to her. Emily was always the smart one," Beaumont said. "The only one who got away."

Cordell watched him drag Raine up the stairs, the gun to her temple. He didn't dare try to stop Beaumont.

Just as Beaumont reached the top, he swung the gun barrel away from Raine's temple and fired back down the stairs. Cordell dove, but not fast enough.

BILL MADE RAINE DRIVE, all the time holding the gun on her. She'd known when he hadn't killed her the moment they stepped out of the old house that he was taking her to where he'd hidden Lara.

She thought she would die at just the thought of Cordell lying, bleeding in that basement. She'd called his name as she was being dragged out of the house, the gun again to her head, but Cordell hadn't answered.

He's not dead. She would know if he was, she would feel it.

Of course, he hadn't answered when she'd called

his name because Bill might have gone back to finish him off.

Think of Lara. Once Lara was safe…

As she drove down to the highway and, following his instructions, turned onto it, Bill pulled out his cell phone. She could hear the phone ringing. Once, twice, three times before it was finally answered.

"I need you to meet me. You know where." He swore. "You're what?" He swore again and barked into the phone, "Damn it, Adele. Don't do anything until I get there. We're on our way." He snapped the phone shut and glared over at her. "This is all your fault."

Did he really believe that? Apparently so. She wanted to argue the fact, but she feared he'd lose his temper and kill her beside the road. He'd already gotten in a few punches. She could feel her left eye threatening to swell shut and her ribs hurt where he'd gotten her with an elbow.

Bill looked worse than she did, she thought. His face was scratched and bleeding when the slats of the crate had connected with it. His nose looked broken. He kept wiping it with his sleeve, glaring at her since it must have hurt.

Raine drove down the deserted highway, trying to focus only on saving Lara and getting back to that house by the river. *Hang in, Cordell.* It was the wee hours of the morning and there didn't seem to be another soul alive in the entire world.

As she drove, though, Raine memorized the way so she could return as soon as Lara was safe.

But Bill's phone call troubled her. The woman he'd called Adele was obviously with Lara—just as Raine had suspected. So why had Bill been surprised by that?

Because if Cordell hadn't shown up when he did, Bill would be taking Orville Cline to Lara now. Adele wasn't supposed to be there. Was it possible she had gone there to free the girl?

"So is Adele your wife?" she asked.

He didn't answer for a moment and she was thinking of asking another question when he said, "Thirty-six years of marital bliss."

Raine shot him a look to see if he was serious. She must have looked surprise to find that he seemed to be because he demanded, "What?"

"I just thought you must not be happy in your marriage if you have to steal little girls and—"

"I don't molest them," he snapped. "What do you think I am?"

She thought he really didn't want to go there. She checked her words. "Then I guess I don't understand why you—"

"No, you don't understand. I love children. I only take the ones who need me." He swore, seeing that she still wasn't getting it. "I wanted children but Adele couldn't have any. I didn't want someone else's child so adoption was out of the question."

"So you pick up children to satisfy your temporary need for a child." Raine couldn't believe what a sick bastard he was.

"You make it sound dirty," he snapped. "But it's not.

I'm good to them. I show them probably the only love they get. It's not my fault that it is only for a short time. They become demanding after a while. They no longer appreciate what I've done for them. They want to go home." His tone had turned nasty.

Raine stole a look and saw that he'd become angry. She didn't dare open her mouth for fear of what she might say.

He glanced behind them as he had several times since they'd hit the highway and mumbled that he should have made sure that bastard was dead or at least disabled the car Orville Cline had stolen.

Raine hadn't dared look back. But from Bill's satisfied expression she knew there were no headlights behind them. That, however, didn't mean that Cordell wasn't alive and following them at this very moment with his headlights turned off.

She prayed that was the case because she needed it to be so. She needed to believe that Cordell was all right—because once they reached wherever Lara English was being kept, Raine knew she was going to need all the help she could get.

Chapter Fifteen

From the floor, the sheriff stared for a moment at the woman holding the knife to Lara English's throat. There was a wild, inhuman look in Adele's eyes that glowed in the lantern light.

McCall slowly dropped her gun.

Adele smiled. "Now don't get up. Just kick the gun over here."

She did as she was ordered and kicked the gun over to Adele. McCall had left her shotgun outside against the door. She hadn't wanted to scare Lara. She looked at the little girl. She seemed calm again. Earlier she'd cried when it looked as if she might be saved. Now she seemed to know better.

"Lara, sweetheart," Adele said as the pistol came to a stop at her feet. "I'm going to put you down. I want you to hand the gun to Mommy. But be really careful."

"Yes, Mommy," Lara said in a robotic voice that tore out McCall's heart—the same thing she wanted to do to Adele Beaumont.

Lara knelt down slowly, the blade pressing against

her small throat, and picked up the pistol. "Here, Mommy."

"Thank you, sweetheart. You are such a good girl," Adele said, as she took the gun in her left hand. She made the exchange from the knife to the gun too quickly for McCall to do anything more than watch. The gun was now pointed at the back of Lara's head.

Lara gave a small brave smile.

"Now," Adele said, holding Lara's arm and the gun to the child's head, "the first thing we are going to do is walk over and take the sheriff's pretty handcuffs. Don't move, Sheriff. You don't want this poor child to die, do you?"

McCall pulled out her handcuffs and handed them to Lara.

"Snap one on the sheriff's wrist. That a girl. Now let me." Adele grabbed the handcuffs, letting go of Lara just long enough to snap the other end of the cuffs to a pipe protruding from the wall.

"Now we're going to walk out to the car and Mommy is going to take you someplace nice for dinner. Are you hungry?"

Lara nodded enthusiastically.

"That's my girl."

The exchange turned McCall's stomach. She couldn't stand the thought of Adele leaving with that child. "Adele, don't do this."

Lara looked concerned again. The prospect of food was too much for her and McCall wondered how long it had been since she'd eaten.

"Do what? Sheriff, I'm a hero. I found Lara and now I'm taking her back to town for a hero's welcome. I tried to tell you that's what I was doing, but you wouldn't listen."

McCall felt sick to her stomach. But as long as Lara was safe.

Adele's smile could have ripped flesh. "In fact, I think I might tell everyone that I caught you here with the little girl. You were about to do something horrible to her. If I hadn't stopped you…"

"No one will believe that."

"Of course they will. I'm Adele Beaumont. Do I look like a woman who would hurt a defenseless child?" She backed toward the front door, still holding the gun to Lara's head. "And by the time I get this child back to town, I know Lara will back up my story. Won't you, Lara. Didn't Mommy come to save you?" The girl nodded obediently. "The poor child has been through so much. She seems to think I'm her mommy. Isn't that sweet?"

"TURN HERE."

Raine slowed and turned down the narrow dirt lane. Ahead she could make out a house sitting in a stand of old cottonwoods. The house looked even more run-down than the one that she'd been held in but a light glowed inside.

There was a large newer model SUV parked on the back side, Raine saw as she pulled in front of the house and stopped. Bill shut off the engine and took the keys.

He glanced back over his shoulder. Still no sign of anyone behind them.

He turned back around just in time to see what Raine saw: a woman coming out of the house with a little girl. Raine barely recognized the child as Lara English. Her hair was matted, her face smudged with dirt and she was wearing a jean jacket that swam on her and apparently little else.

In the light that spilled from the open door of the house, Raine looked from Lara to the woman holding the girl's hand and felt her heart drop. *You can call me Mommy.* Her earlier fear seized her at the sight of the horrible woman who'd been part of her abduction sixteen years ago.

Beside her, Bill swore. "Damn that woman. She's going to mess everything up." He threw open his door, then seemed to remember Raine. "Get out," he ordered, brandishing the gun.

Raine climbed out and when she did she saw something that made her heart soar. A glint of light from the moon reflecting off what had to have been a vehicle. It disappeared over a rise in the road Raine had just driven up. She listened for a moment but didn't hear the sound of a car engine. Could she have just imagined—

Bill grabbed her arm and shoved her toward the house. "Get back inside, Adele. Now!"

Adele had stopped beside her car. The door was open and she'd apparently just dragged out a jacket from the back. As she slipped into it, she watched her husband thoughtfully. Raine could tell the woman was thinking about trying to make a run for it with the girl. Would her husband of thirty-six years shoot her?

"Adele." The warning in his tone seemed to force Adele's decision. She grabbed Lara more roughly and pushed her toward the house.

Lara entered with Adele behind her. Raine followed, Bill with his gun on her.

He seemed to notice the sheriff handcuffed to a pipe about the same time as Raine. "What the hell, Adele?" he demanded. "What is the sheriff doing here?"

Raine watched Adele seem to shrink under Bill's anger. "She must have followed me from town," she said in a small, childlike voice.

"You think?" He turned on her and Adele shrank away from him. "You just never learn, do you, Adele? Now I'm going to have to clean up the mess you made. Just like I always have to do."

CORDELL HAD BANDAGED his side as best he could but it was bleeding again as he got out of the car. He'd searched Orville Cline's body for the keys the moment he'd heard Beaumont's truck engine turn over.

Now he followed a small gully toward the house where he'd seen Beaumont's truck stop. He had to stop once to adjust the makeshift bandage he'd constructed out of an old sweatshirt he'd found in the car. The sweatshirt said Montana State University across the front. Now it was wet with blood.

He moved through the trees that once sheltered the house in time to see a woman and child go inside, followed by Raine with Beaumont close behind holding a gun on her.

As he neared the edge of the house, he saw something by the door glint in the moonlight. Stepping closer, he saw that it was a shotgun.

Inside the house, he heard Beaumont's raised voice. He seemed to be hollering at his wife.

Cordell plucked up the shotgun and moved quickly back from the open doorway to check to make sure it was loaded.

It was.

Then he moved toward the door again. The last thing he'd heard Bill Beaumont say was something about cleaning up his wife's messes. Life, Cordell thought, was all about timing.

He knew he would have the advantage of surprise, but he would also have only an instant to assess the situation and act. He would be jeopardizing Raine's and Lara's lives. Unfortunately there was no one else here to rectify things and he was losing blood and wasn't sure how much longer he'd be standing.

He prayed for perfect timing as he rounded the doorway, leading with the shotgun.

RAINE WAS NEVER SO HAPPY to see anyone come through that doorway. She felt such a well of emotion to see that Cordell was alive. If she'd ever doubted it, she knew now. She loved this man.

Bill had taken his eyes off her just moments before to go over and berate his wife. Raine had taken advantage of his inattention and pulled Lara over to her. The girl came willing enough. She seemed dazed, lost, and Raine recognized that look and felt sick inside that this child had had to go through what she'd experienced.

And suddenly Cordell appeared in the doorway with the shotgun. Adele saw him and let out a cry to warn Bill.

Raine acted on instinct, shoving Lara in the direction of the sheriff as Bill spun around. McCall grabbed the girl and covered her head as the sound of the shotgun blast boomed.

The boom reverberated through the old house. Bill made a gurgling sound, stumbling backward. Cordell suddenly seemed to be having trouble standing and Raine realized he'd been shot earlier just as she'd feared.

He took a step toward her, then dropped to one knee. A wadded-up piece of clothing fell from inside his jacket. Raine's heart dropped at the sight of the blood-soaked material.

As she started to rush to Cordell, she saw Adele trying to get the gun from her jacket pocket.

"Cordell, watch out!" she cried as she dove for Adele, slamming her back against the wall.

Adele had managed to get the gun from her pocket. Raine grabbed the gun, trying to wrench it from the woman's hands, but Adele was much stronger than she looked.

McCALL HELD THE GIRL to her as she worked with her foot to get the pistol that Bill Beaumont had dropped when he was shot. She finally got a boot toe around it and dragged it back toward her.

She could see Raine trying to wrest the gun from Adele, but she knew only too well how strong Adele was. That strength came from that inhuman part of her, McCall thought, as she dragged the gun to her.

Letting go of Lara, she grabbed up the gun with her free hand and fired two quick shots. Neither seemed to have any effect on Adele for a few moments.

McCall prepared to fire again when she saw Adele's fingers slip from the gun she was fighting to keep from Raine. The woman glanced over at her, a horrible hateful look in her eyes, before she looked down at where the bullets had torn through her jacket. The cloth blossomed red as Adele Beaumont slowly slid to the floor.

Leaning back, McCall laid the gun next to her and pulled Lara close again. Past Lara, Raine rushed to Cordell to press the wet cloth to his side.

Lara sat up as if sensing it was over. "I'm hungry," she said.

McCall started to tell Raine to go down the road to her patrol SUV to call for backup but before she could two deputies burst in followed by one very good-looking game warden.

"Adele has the key to the cuffs in her pocket," McCall said as Luke Crawford started to rush to her.

He went to the fallen woman and came back with the key. As he unlocked the cuffs, he sat down next to McCall on the floor and pulled her to him.

"How did you—?"

"Shane told me where you were when you called in the last time," Luke said. "I remembered this old farmhouse. I know we were supposed to wait for your call, but when we didn't hear from you…"

She smiled up at him, then pulled him down for a kiss. What would she ever do without this man?

Across the room, one of the deputies was seeing to Cordell as they waited for the ambulance to arrive. Another deputy had given Lara a stick of gum, promising her a candy bar once they reached his patrol car.

McCall leaned into Luke, absorbing his warmth. "I should have followed my first instinct and shot her right away. I sure wanted to."

Luke pulled her closer. "But you didn't."

No, she thought as she looked across the room to where Adele Beaumont lay, all the crazy wild gone from her blank eyes. "But I'm not sorry she's dead. I'm not sorry they're both dead. How is Cordell though?"

Luke shook his head. "He's apparently lost a lot of blood, but the ambulance is on the way."

Chapter Sixteen

Raine stepped into Cordell's hospital room. It was right down the hall from his brother Cyrus's. Her relief and joy at hearing that Cordell was going to pull through was tempered with the news that Cyrus's condition hadn't changed.

As she neared his bed, Cordell opened those wonderful dark eyes of his and smiled. His face, though pale, seemed to light up and she felt weightless and silly and ecstatic. Tears welled in her eyes as he reached for her hand and pulled her closer.

She leaned her face against his and tried not to cry.

"Hey," he said. "I'm okay."

She nodded through her tears.

"You were amazing."

Raine didn't feel amazing. She'd endangered all of their lives.

"How's Lara?" he asked.

"Good." Drying her eyes and pulling herself together, she told him about the deputies taking her out for breakfast at the Great Northern. "She put down pancakes, eggs and bacon without blinking an eye. It turns out that the girl's grandmother saw the story on the news. Apparently, she'd lost contact with her daughter and granddaughter. McCall is helping her get custody. Lara is very excited since she has happy memories of staying with her grandmother when she was younger."

"That is good news," Cordell said.

She heard the change in his voice. "Cyrus is still stable."

He nodded. "I know. I'd hoped that by the time this was over, he would be back with us."

"I'm so sorry," Raine said, her voice breaking. "This is all my fault."

"Baby, this is the Beaumonts' fault and Orville Cline's. But they are all gone now, may they never rest in hell." He stroked her hair. "If it hadn't been for you, Lara would have been another casualty of those monsters."

Raine laid her head on his chest and listened to the steady beat of his heart.

"I need to tell you how I feel about you, Raine."

She lifted her head, afraid of what he was going to say, afraid he didn't feel the way she did.

"No, I won't let you stop me this time," he said before she could speak. "I love you. I know this is sudden and you probably don't feel the same way but—"

Raine smiled through fresh tears as she touched a finger to his lips. "I feel the same way."

He laughed, then grimaced at the pain. "You do?"

"I do."

He grinned. "Those are words I'd like to hear you say one of these days real soon."

Epilogue

McCall was amazed how quickly life had gone back to normal. Her first calls had been the usual White-horse crimes: complaints about barking dogs and loud teenagers, requests to make checks on the elderly and giving rides home from the bars to those who weren't able to drive.

She'd come down from the shock of the events of the past few weeks. Cousin Cyrus was still in a coma, but he was stable and they were all holding out hope he would regain consciousness at any time.

Fortunately her cousin Cordell had recovered nicely, Lara had been placed with her grandmother until a permanent custody could be arranged and even the gossip had died down somewhat about the Beaumonts.

Other than that, life seemed to be getting back to normal, well, as normal as it could in Whitehorse, Montana.

Then her cell phone rang and she saw that it was her grandmother.

"Good morning, Grandmother," McCall said. It still seemed strange to call Pepper Winchester Grandmother.

She'd gone all twenty-seven years of her life with Pepper denying her existence.

But all that was behind them and even McCall's mother, Ruby, was starting to come around. Ruby was actually looking forward to her daughter's Christmas wedding at Winchester Ranch.

"I just talked to the local florist," her grandmother was saying. "She said you hadn't been over to look at flowers for the wedding. Tell me you've at least ordered your dress. You do realize the wedding isn't that far away?"

"It's June and the wedding isn't until Christmas."

"Exactly. You can't keep putting this off. Tomorrow I could have Enid drive me in—"

"That's not necessary," McCall said.

"I know, but I'd like to help you. That is, if it's all right with your mother."

She heard the plea in her grandmother's voice. "I would love it if you'd come with me to pick out the flowers."

There was a lightness to her grandmother's voice that McCall hadn't heard before. "When's a good time?"

"We could meet at Jan's Floral at noon," McCall suggested. "Would that work for you?"

"That would be perfect. Maybe we could have lunch afterward. That is if you don't have to get back to work right away."

McCall smiled, listening to how formal they sounded. "That would be nice."

"Thank you. Would Luke like to join us?"

"To pick out flowers?" Her game warden fiancé would have no interest in picking out flowers for the wedding. Luke had been great, though, about having the wedding at the ranch.

"You deserve to have your wedding there," he'd said. "You're a Winchester and it's high time everyone accepted it. Also I suspect it's your grandmother's way to trying to make amends."

McCall hoped that was the case and that her grandmother wasn't using the wedding as part of one of her hidden agendas.

"Luke's working down in the Missouri Breaks," she told her grandmother now. "It's fishing season, you know. Lots of licenses to check."

"All right then. I will see you tomorrow." Pepper sounded as if she wanted to say more but McCall got another call and had to let her go. Whatever it was, McCall figured she'd find out soon enough. Hopefully *before* the wedding.

CORDELL SAT DOWN NEXT to his brother's bed and took Cyrus's hand in his. That twin connection that had always been there was still gone and he felt such a weight on his chest that sometimes he couldn't breathe.

"We got the bad guys," he said quietly. "Just as I promised. I sure could have used your help though. Now it's time for you to come back."

The only sound in the room was the beep of the monitor.

Cyrus was still alive. That meant there was hope.

Cordell latched on to that slim thread and held on for dear life.

"I can't wait to tell you about Raine. You're going to love her. The two of you met already." He swallowed, feeling the burn of tears and fought them back. "She's a lot like you. Brave to a fault and she's a private investigator. Can you beat that?"

Cordell realized how foolish he'd been to think that once he caught the people responsible that Cyrus would wake up.

It had been crazy. Cyrus's condition hadn't changed since the accident. It might never change.

He shoved that thought away and stood as the doctor came into the room. Cordell knew he had to make a decision. He followed the doctor out into the hall.

"You have to face the possibility that your brother might never recover from his injury," the doctor said again.

Cordell nodded, though he doubted he could ever accept that.

"I would suggest moving him to a long-term care facility that specializes in these kinds of cases."

"I want to take him back to Colorado. Is there a problem with transporting him in his condition?"

"He is breathing on his own, his vitals are strong, I see no problem with that and there are some fine facilities in Denver."

Cordell nodded. "I'll make arrangements right away then."

"ARE YOU LEAVING?" Pepper Winchester asked in surprise.

Her daughter Virginia turned from packing clothing into her suitcase, her expression sour. "There is no reason to stay here under the circumstances."

"The circumstances being that your mother isn't dying quickly enough?"

"Mother, don't start," Virginia said. "You don't want or need me here. You have Enid. She is more like a daughter to you than I am."

Pepper couldn't hold back the laugh. "Enid?"

"Fine. If not Enid then definitely Brand and the others."

"Oh, Virginia, must you always come back to this?" Behind her, Pepper heard Brand and Worth come up the hall. They were carrying their overnight bags. Apparently they were all leaving.

What surprised her was how hollow that made her feel. She didn't want them to go. She realized how incongruous that was since she still believed one of them was an accomplice to murder.

"I'll let you say goodbye to your brothers," Pepper said and, cane tapping, went down the hall where she found Enid eavesdropping. She stopped next to the elderly housekeeper, who didn't seem the least bit upset about being caught.

Even though she knew what would be said about her and how much it would hurt, Pepper stayed there by Enid to listen.

"Why *did* she get us back here?" Virginia demanded

in her shrill voice. "She really can't believe that one of us had something to do with Trace's death."

"I don't know," Brand said and sighed. "Maybe she needs us."

Worth swore. "A little late, don't you think?"

"He's right, Mother never needed anyone but Trace," Virginia said, close to tears.

"I think you're smart to leave," Brand said, always the sensible one. "Being here just seems to bring back all those old resentments."

Pepper could almost hear her daughter bristle.

"Don't pretend I'm the only one who can't forgive Mother."

"Virginia, I really don't want to get into this," Brand said. "I have one son recovering from gunshot wounds and another in a coma. I'm much more concerned about the future than I am the past."

"At least you have children," Virginia spat.

In the silence that followed Pepper could hear what none of them could bring themselves to say. Pepper knew they were all thinking about the child Virginia had given birth to and lost.

"Virginia," Brand said, clearly trying to be diplomatic. "You didn't have anything to do with Trace's—"

"Is that what you think? That I had something to do with killing him?" Virginia let out a laugh.

"You knew the woman who confessed to killing him."

"So did you. So did Worth and Angus, not to mention Enid and Alfred. Who said it had to be one of us?"

"She's right," Worth spoke up. "Alfred might be dead, but Enid doesn't appear to be going anywhere and any fool can see that something is going on between Enid and Mother. If I had to guess I'd say blackmail. I wouldn't put it past Enid for an instant."

Beside Pepper, Enid let out a snort and whispered, "I never liked that boy."

"I'm sure it will all sort itself out," Brand said. "Who says the woman didn't lie about one of us being involved?"

"Oh, that is so like you, Brand," Virginia snapped. "You always just put your head into the sand and pretend everything is fine. Sort itself out. In other words, you're not going to do a damned thing, are you?"

"What would you like me to do? I can't change Mother and I can't change the past. What is it you want me to do, Virginia? Just tell me and I'll do it."

Virginia was crying again.

Pepper heard Worth and Brand start down the hall. She and Enid hurriedly took the servants' stairs to the kitchen.

"Mother?" Brand called when they reached the front entry.

Pepper came out of the kitchen to tell her sons goodbye. Virginia joined them, sans suitcase. Apparently she'd changed her mind about leaving.

"Are you coming back for the wedding at Christmas?" Pepper asked them after she'd given her sons both awkward hugs.

Worth merely nodded, expressing what Pepper knew

to be true of him. He would come back if the others did. It was as if he didn't have a mind of his own and never had. She sighed inwardly.

"Are you sure it's a good idea to have the wedding here?" Virginia asked. "I know McCall's the sheriff and her fiancé is some kind of law enforcement, but they aren't bulletproof and Winchester Ranch doesn't seem to be the safest place."

Pepper ignored her as she looked to Brand. The others would do whatever he did. Until that moment, she hadn't realized just how much this meant to her to have them all here. Sentiment aside, there was still a murderer among them. If it was on her last dying breath, she would know which one it was.

"I'll be here," Brand said as if he had a bad feeling he'd better come home for Christmas this year.

RAINE HAD JUST PICKED UP her VW bug at the garage when Cordell drove up in his brother's pickup. It was one of those Montana summer days, not a cloud in the brilliant blue sky, the sun bright and warm, the breeze scented with freshly mown grass.

She watched him from the shade of the building as he climbed out, still taken aback that this gorgeous man loved *her*.

Raine realized for the first time she wasn't worried about the future. For sixteen years, she'd lived with the knowledge that there were people out there who would kill her if they knew who she really was. She hadn't been able to forget for even a minute that she was Emily Frank, the victim of child abductors.

But as Cordell Winchester came toward her, she realized she was Raine Chandler, a woman who could finally dream of a happily ever after.

"Hi, beautiful," Cordell said now as he took her in his arms and kissed her. He held her tight and she could tell he didn't like even a temporary separation. But he had to take care of his brother and she had to discuss with Marias selling her half of their investigative business in California.

Last night, lying out on a blanket under the Montana midnight sky, Cordell had asked her to marry him. She'd told him it was too soon. He'd argued that some things you just knew for certain and this was something he just knew and more time together wouldn't change his mind.

So she'd made him a deal. They would get married when Cyrus was able to be the best man at the wedding. Cordell's eyes had filled with tears. He'd started to ask but what if Cyrus never—

Raine had stopped him. "That's the deal," she'd said. In the meantime, they would take care of business and see each other as often as they could.

"Promise me I'll see you in Colorado soon," Cordell said now as the kiss ended.

She gazed into his dark eyes, felt her heart fill to overflowing with love for this man, and whispered back, "I promise."

* * * * *

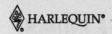
HARLEQUIN®

INTRIGUE

COMING NEXT MONTH

Available July 13, 2010

#1215 GUARDING GRACE
Bodyguard of the Month
Rebecca York

#1216 COLBY CONTROL
Colby Agency: Merger
Debra Webb

#1217 THE MOMMY MYSTERY
Texas Maternity: Hostages
Delores Fossen

#1218 UNBREAKABLE BOND
Guardian Angel Investigations
Rita Herron

#1219 KEEPING WATCH
Shivers
Jan Hambright

**#1220 A RANCHER'S BRAND
OF JUSTICE**
Ann Voss Peterson

HICNM0610

REQUEST YOUR FREE BOOKS!

2 FREE NOVELS PLUS 2 FREE GIFTS!

Breathtaking Romantic Suspense

YES! Please send me 2 FREE Harlequin Intrigue® novels and my 2 FREE gifts (gifts are worth about $10). After receiving them, if I don't wish to receive any more books, I can return the shipping statement marked "cancel." If I don't cancel, I will receive 6 brand-new novels every month and be billed just $4.24 per book in the U.S. or $4.99 per book in Canada. That's a saving of at least 15% off the cover price! It's quite a bargain! Shipping and handling is just 50¢ per book.* I understand that accepting the 2 free books and gifts places me under no obligation to buy anything. I can always return a shipment and cancel at any time. Even if I never buy another book from Harlequin, the two free books and gifts are mine to keep forever.

182/382 HDN E5MG

Name _____ (PLEASE PRINT)

Address _____ Apt. #

City _____ State/Prov. _____ Zip/Postal Code

Signature (if under 18, a parent or guardian must sign)

Mail to the Harlequin Reader Service:
IN U.S.A.: P.O. Box 1867, Buffalo, NY 14240-1867
IN CANADA: P.O. Box 609, Fort Erie, Ontario L2A 5X3

Not valid for current subscribers to Harlequin Intrigue books.

Are you a subscriber to Harlequin Intrigue books and want to receive the larger-print edition? Call 1-800-873-8635 today!

* Terms and prices subject to change without notice. Prices do not include applicable taxes. N.Y. residents add applicable sales tax. Canadian residents will be charged applicable provincial taxes and GST. Offer not valid in Quebec. This offer is limited to one order per household. All orders subject to approval. Credit or debit balances in a customer's account(s) may be offset by any other outstanding balance owed by or to the customer. Please allow 4 to 6 weeks for delivery. Offer available while quantities last.

Your Privacy: Harlequin is committed to protecting your privacy. Our Privacy Policy is available online at www.eHarlequin.com or upon request from the Reader Service. From time to time we make our lists of customers available to reputable third parties who may have a product or service of interest to you. If you would prefer we not share your name and address, please check here. ☐

Help us get it right—We strive for accurate, respectful and relevant communications. To clarify or modify your communication preferences, visit us at www.ReaderService.com/consumerschoice.

H11OR

HARLEQUIN®

A *Romance*

FOR EVERY MOOD™

Spotlight on

── Heart & Home ──

Heartwarming romances
where love can happen
right when you least expect it.

See the next page to enjoy a sneak peek
from Silhouette Special Edition®,
a Heart and Home series.

*Introducing McFARLANE'S PERFECT BRIDE
by* USA TODAY *bestselling author Christine Rimmer,
from Silhouette Special Edition®.*

Entranced. Captivated. Enchanted.

Connor sat across the table from Tori Jones and couldn't help thinking that those words exactly described what effect the small-town schoolteacher had on him. He might as well stop trying to tell himself he wasn't interested. He was powerfully drawn to her.

Clearly, he should have dated more when he was younger.

There had been a couple of other women since Jennifer had walked out on him. But he had never been entranced. Or captivated. Or enchanted.

Until now.

He wanted her—*her,* Tori Jones, in particular. Not just someone suitably attractive and well-bred, as Jennifer had been. Not just someone sophisticated, sexually exciting and discreet, which pretty much described the two women he'd dated after his marriage crashed and burned.

It came to him that he…he *liked* this woman. And that was new to him. He liked her quick wit, her wisdom and her big heart. He liked the passion in her voice when she talked about things she believed in.

He liked *her.* And suddenly it mattered all out of proportion that she might like him, too.

Was he losing it? He couldn't help but wonder. Was he cracking under the strain—of the soured economy, the McFarlane House setbacks, his divorce, the scary changes in his son? Of the changes he'd decided he needed to make in his life and himself?

Strangely, right then, on his first date with Tori Jones, he didn't care if he just might be going over the edge. He was having a great time—having *fun,* of all things—and he didn't want it to end.

Is Connor finally able to admit his feelings to Tori,
and are they reciprocated?
Find out in McFARLANE'S PERFECT BRIDE
by USA TODAY *bestselling author Christine Rimmer.*
Available July 2010,
only from Silhouette Special Edition®.

Silhouette *Desire*

USA TODAY bestselling author

MAUREEN CHILD

brings you the first
of a six-book miniseries—
Dynasties: The Jarrods

Book one:
CLAIMING HER BILLION-DOLLAR BIRTHRIGHT

Erica Prentice has set out to claim
her billion-dollar inheritance
and the man she loves.

*Available in July
wherever you buy books.*

Always Powerful, Passionate and Provocative.

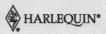

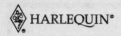
HARLEQUIN®

Showcase

On sale June 8

Reader favorites from the most talented voices in romance

Save $1.00 on the purchase of 1 or more Harlequin® Showcase books.

SAVE $1.00 on the purchase of 1 or more Harlequin® Showcase books.

Coupon expires November 30, 2010. Redeemable at participating retail outlets.
Limit one coupon per customer. Valid in the U.S.A. and Canada only.

Canadian Retailers: Harlequin Enterprises Limited will pay the face value of this coupon plus 10.25¢ if submitted by customer for this product only. Any other use constitutes fraud. Coupon is nonassignable. Void if taxed, prohibited or restricted by law. Consumer must pay any government taxes. Void if copied. Nielsen Clearing House ("NCH") customers submit coupons and proof of sales to Harlequin Enterprises Limited, P.O. Box 3000, Saint John, NB E2L 4L3, Canada. Non-NCH retailer—for reimbursement submit coupons and proof of sales directly to Harlequin Enterprises Limited, Retail Marketing Department, 225 Duncan Mill Rd., Don Mills, ON M3B 3K9, Canada.

52609057

U.S. Retailers: Harlequin Enterprises Limited will pay the face value of this coupon plus 8¢ if submitted by customer for this product only. Any other use constitutes fraud. Coupon is nonassignable. Void if taxed, prohibited or restricted by law. Consumer must pay any government taxes. Void if copied. For reimbursement submit coupons and proof of sales directly to Harlequin Enterprises Limited, P.O. Box 880478, El Paso, TX 88588-0478, U.S.A. Cash value 1/100 cents.

5 65373 00076 2   (8100)0 11654

® and TM are trademarks owned and used by the trademark owner and/or its licensee.
© 2010 Harlequin Enterprises Limited

HSCCOUP0610